One glance, and everything changed.

Connor turned away to check out the big red brick high school and stopped. He was surprised and a little embarrassed to realize his jaw had actually dropped, but that didn't change the effect.

An absolutely gorgeous woman walked toward them, with a smile brighter than the leaves on all those autumn trees.

She was around his age, and moved with all the strength and confidence he'd ever seen from women in the city and more.

The early evening sun seemed to start a fire all its own in her curly blonde hair, caught back in a bouncy ponytail that struck Connor as a real shame.

He wanted to see her hair loose and falling around her shoulders, shifting with every move of her body.

Every *breath*.

He shook his head, not sure where on earth such thoughts could be coming from inside his normally calm and pretty much orderly mind.

But no one had ever struck him so deep and hard on first sight.

Storms of the Heart: A Storms of Future Past Romance

Published 2020 by Spiral Publishing, Ltd.
www.spiralpublishing.net
St. Paul, Virginia

Book and cover design copyright © 2020 by Spiral Publishing, Ltd.

Cover art copyright © 2020 by serezniy | depositphotos.com

ISBN-13: 978-1-948890-53-3
Large Print ISBN-13: 978-1-948890-54-0

For Jason

*Who knows how often paths change
for the better*

STORMS OF THE HEART

A STORMS OF FUTURE PAST ROMANCE

KARI KILGORE

SPIRAL PUBLISHING, LTD.

Chapter 1

THE BIG RECTANGULAR football field behind the sprawling brick high school had been freshly mown, with bright white lines painted every ten yards just that afternoon. All the trees on the mountains rising up behind it on three sides were bursting with autumn color after a few cool nights.

Red, yellow, and orange set off the dark, healthy green of the grass perfectly, and the crisp rustling of the leaves in the cool breeze sounded fantastic.

Laura Michaelson leaned against the rough red brick of the school she'd graduated from four years ago, staring up at the perfect deep blue October sky. She would have known it was her favorite time of year from the smells alone back there.

Besides the fresh-cut grass, she caught traces of a wood fire from somewhere close by. The one-story brick building across the wide parking lot between the school and the field added another distinctive aroma. The long, low building with a distinctive peaked metal roof had the words *Wolf Branch Cannery* painted in fading purple along the front.

Someone inside was cooking apples, maybe for applesauce. Laura couldn't see through the big windows in front from this angle, but the smell was more than enough to get her attention.

She hated the way the cannery had gotten run down over the last ten years or so. Her father talked about how the vast steel pots used for boiling jars or the ranges along the back wall or some other bit of equipment stopped working, and never got repaired.

Neither she nor anyone in her family had the skills or time to do anything about it, though, and most people in Wolf Branch, Virginia, didn't seem to care. Too easy to run down to one of the grocery stores or order whatever anyone could want online.

A handful of cars were parked more or less within the spaces drawn on the faded black asphalt, most of them old enough to still run on gasoline. Laura's little white hatchback was a 2024 model, already three years old itself. But at least it was electric rather than spewing pollution into the mountain air.

The hand-me-down cars probably meant mostly students parked back here this late on a Thursday, just like when Laura was driving her own junker and going to classes. A bunch were still at school for some kind of band practice she could hear off in the distance with staccato snare drums and brassy trumpets. Or they were scattered around inside for debate team practice or a play rehearsal or something equally dramatic and important to life in high school.

No football practice on this field, not with the grass all dressed up and fancy for the big game in a couple of nights. That at least would have been something to watch out here while she waited. With the much-despised rivals from Laurel Gap playing the strongest they had in years, the Wolf Branch team was certainly practicing hard on their secondary field a couple of blocks away.

Laura shook her head, amazed that she knew all of that when she didn't go to school here any more and only rarely attended a game. The awareness floated in the very air of these small mountain towns, a vital part of the social fabric.

She was already good and bored with the three groups of middle-aged men and women walking slowly around the springy brown track around the edge of the field. Walking very, very slowly, so they were probably as old as her parents. Maybe in their forties. Maybe even older.

Laura sighed, pulling her curly blonde ponytail forward over her shoulder. She wasn't exactly old by most people's standards at twenty-two. But compared to those kids inside, playing scales or mock-arguing or rehearsing lines, sometimes she felt absolutely ancient.

Her clothes were close enough to acceptable around here today, or at least they would have been if they were a bit more stylish or maybe more beat up. And anyway, she wasn't here to fit in with a bunch of high schoolers. A pair of new blue jeans and a red button-up shirt would do for the people she was supposed to meet.

People who were later than they'd said they'd be and then some. She resisted the urge to check her watch, but she knew six o'clock had already come and gone.

Sure, they'd only arrived from Chicago last night after what had to be a long, unpleasant drive, bringing all their belongings with them. She'd heard they had family back here or something like that, but Laura still couldn't quite *imagine* why anyone would move from such a big exciting city to a sleepy little town in Appalachia.

Peace and quiet? Oh yeah, this town had that to spare.

Not much else as far as she was concerned, though she

was doing her best to make sure what they did have got better. So here she still was.

A car slowing on the sloping road that passed by the school and the cannery caught her attention. Sure enough, the blue gas-powered sedan turned in and parked in an empty spot in front of the cannery. Whoever was driving at least got it perfectly between the lines.

Laura squinted to make sure, but she couldn't read the license plate on the back well enough to tell whether it was from Illinois. When a man and a woman with hair shot through with silver got out, she walked toward them.

She'd never seen them before, but she did know Anne and Evan Griffith were somewhere in their mid-fifties.

And what the hell, she was here on behalf of the town council and the high school anyway. Might as well greet whoever *had* arrived, even if it wasn't her tardy newcomers.

Laura missed a step and nearly stumbled when a guy her own age got out of the back of the sedan and stretched with his arms over his head. He wasn't as tall as the man who had to be his father, but had the same shape to his face.

But the young guy had the same brown hair as the woman. And even from several paces away, Laura could see how green his eyes were.

No one had mentioned a son her age making the trip. And a very *handsome* son at that. Even better, an exotic son who she assumed had grown up in Chicago.

Jim Blevins, the guy Laura had been dating for the last couple of years, popped up in her mind for a brief second. In their case—and Laura was certain it was true for both of them—familiarity had done nothing at all to keep things lively between them over the last few months.

At least for her part, they were still as together as they were because he was so familiar.

Safe. Predictable.

And maybe because nothing better had come along.

Maybe not until now.

The dull prospect of this little meet and greet brightened considerably, along with Laura's mood.

And her smile.

Chapter 2

Connor Griffith unfolded himself out of his parents' sedan and stretched as tall as he could, groaning as his cramped muscles shifted and relaxed. They'd made the drive down from Chicago several times while he was growing up, so he should have been used to it.

The back seat of what had to be the last new production model car that ran on gasoline was plenty spacious enough, he had to give it that. But sitting back there for ten hours with only a couple of stops left him achy and sore.

Apparently his deciding to skip it for the last few years had eroded his road trip tolerance.

That or he was prematurely old and creaky at a positively ancient twenty-five.

Deciding to ride with them rather than drive himself made plenty of sense a couple of weeks ago. No sense putting even more miles on his already battered work truck, especially when it wasn't exactly built for comfort to begin with.

Renting a nice, new sedan for the return trip sounded like fun, too.

All the hours on the road—with his parents wanting to get here fast rather than stopping more than they had to— left him wishing more than once for his own ride.

Even with all those visits over the years, the mountains jutting up behind the flat space of the pretty little football field looked strange to his eyes. The fall color was much brighter and more vivid than back in Chicago, too. The difference in getting several hours further southeast was startling this time of year.

An especially warm fall with hardly any rain had left most of the leaves up north simply turning brown and falling off, even as they'd driven southeast all day long into more forested countryside in Illinois and Indiana. The trees in Kentucky, though, and here in Virginia, were like moving fire. Sounded a bit like a crackling campfire, too, as the leaves shifted and danced in a cool breeze that felt like heaven against his skin.

The air smelled fantastic down here in the mountains, better than he remembered. Fresh and crisp, with an earthy, warm scent he couldn't identify, and another he knew for certain. He missed the constantly changing smells of the big lake, but he'd be back there soon enough.

After a quick glance to make sure his parents were out and moving around, he pulled out his phone and tapped a quick message to his girlfriend back home, letting her know they'd made it to Wolf Branch.

Well, *girlfriend* might be a little strong for what he had going with Trish.

Special friend, maybe? *Extra* friend? Or he could fall back on the shockingly old-fashioned and terribly embarrassing term his mother used when they'd talked about his situation on the drive down.

Friends with benefits.

Connor shook his head, determined that they were finished talking about him and Trish until there was something new to talk about. Which there wouldn't be until he got back to Chicago and they continued trying to figure it all out.

The happiest couple he knew or had ever heard of seemed like a strange choice to dissect his rather uneventful love life, anyway.

He'd dated on and off for ten years, sure. A couple of his breakups had been dramatic, yes. But not especially life-changing. Not like what he'd heard about in stories of his parents.

The two of them had been in love pretty much since birth, and that showed no signs of slowing now that they were in their fifties. As he watched, his father put his arm around his mother, then leaned down and kissed the top of her head.

A few of what his mom called sparkles showed in her brown hair, but it was mostly still the same color as Connor's. Streaks of silver were more visible in his dad's black hair, but he still had the same curiosity and enthusiasm for everything around him as ever.

And both of them would have laughed and laughed—lines deepening around his dad's pale blue eyes and his mom's green—if Connor had dared breathe a word of thinking either one of them were even in the neighborhood of old.

He mostly appreciated their insistence on being honest and open about his mother's…odd dreams and visions and such. The way they'd both started talking about this move for months before his father got the opportunity for early retirement from teaching at the university. How they'd found the perfect house online almost the instant it went for sale. A house they'd both been inside, but never talked to the owners about buying.

Too many things to mention, and all too reliably correct to doubt. Connor had always known about all of that, and how it had affected his mom's whole life.

What he didn't know, what both of them were extremely careful to make sure he *never* knew, was anything about himself. His own future. Never a blurted out warning or unusual encouragement.

Once in a while, like when it came to Trish, he wished they'd give out the occasional tidbit.

He turned away from them to check out the big red brick high school and stopped. He was surprised and a little embarrassed to realize his jaw had actually dropped, but that didn't change the effect.

An absolutely gorgeous woman walked toward them, with a smile brighter than the leaves on all those autumn trees.

She was around his age, and moved with all the strength and confidence he'd ever seen from women in the city and more.

The early evening sun seemed to start a fire all its own in her curly blonde hair, caught back in a bouncy ponytail that struck Connor as a real shame. He wanted to see her hair loose and falling around her shoulders, shifting with every move of her body. Every *breath*.

He shook his head, not sure where on earth such thoughts could be coming from inside his normally calm and pretty much orderly mind.

But no one had ever struck him so deep and hard on first sight. Not even Trish.

Definitely not Trish.

"Anne?" she said holding her hand out. "Evan? I'm Laura Michaelson, so glad to meet you."

And her voice…

Smooth and rich and deeper than he expected, with a

soft, musical lilt to her words. So different from the long vowels and clipped words, the nasal voices he was used to up north.

His mother held out her own hand with a big grin, as if she were meeting a long-lost best friend.

"I'm *delighted* to meet you, Laura, and I'm so sorry we're late. Had a little bit of trouble getting organized out at our house."

"That's fine, I understand. Moving can be more of a challenge than you expect." She switched to shaking hands with Connor's father, and shot more than one pointed glance Connor's way.

"This is our son Connor," his dad said, with an odd little smile of his own. "Made the trip to help us get settled in. He'll be heading back up north in a week or so."

Connor tried not to grimace or scowl at his father's words. Never mind that they were true.

The beautiful woman—Laura—took his hand and stared into his eyes for a second. Hers were a lovely shade of blue, much darker than his father's.

"Nice to meet you, Connor," she said, still holding his hand. "Shame you'll be leaving us so soon."

"Well, you know," he said. "Sometimes these things are flexible."

His phone and watch buzzed, and even having them both set to silent didn't stop Laura and his parents from glancing at his wrist. Connor didn't have to look to know who the message was from.

"I'll let you attend to that," Laura said, dropping his hand. "I understand you're interested in doing a bit of teaching here, Evan? And Anne, we're delighted to welcome an expert librarian to Wolf Branch."

Connor tried to ignore how cold his hand felt after Laura let go. How strangely *lonely*.

He turned away, trying even harder to ignore how the message from Trish felt like an interruption.

This was going to be a long visit no matter how long he stayed.

Chapter 3

Laura did her best to push down her absurdly strong reaction to speaking with Connor, touching his hand. Reasons why it didn't matter floated through her mind.

He was going back to Chicago, and soon.

She got the strong impression from how he looked at his phone that he wasn't exactly single.

She herself wasn't exactly single, either. Jim might be as bored in their relationship as she was, but that didn't change the fact that they were indeed *in* it.

No, she needed to do her job, welcome their new residents, and move on. The town hadn't hired her before she even finished her degree just to pay her to flirt with unavailable guys.

She'd almost forgotten asking Evan Griffith a question when he answered.

"I'd love to keep teaching, sure. Stay involved for certain. The *early* part of early retirement means I'm not exactly ready to hang everything up and sit around the house."

"Good! We'd be thrilled to have someone with your skills

and qualifications teaching here in Wolf Branch. You teach history, right?"

Evan smiled, and Laura saw the same natural charm that she'd caught in Connor.

Who was now standing off to the side, focusing on his phone, and ignoring everyone else.

Maybe *not* so charming.

"History, sure," Evan said, smiling at his wife. "I do my time with the general classes in U.S. history. Or I should say I did. But I concentrate on the history of agriculture when I can. Pesticides of all kinds, organic and manufactured, and pollinators, how that all works together. Until it doesn't."

Laura rubbed her arms, wondering at the goosebumps running all over them. It wasn't so much what he'd said. More the ominous, somehow final way he'd said it.

Anne seemed to catch her unease, or maybe she'd been just as disturbed by what Evan said.

"I've been here a few times," Anne said, "but I don't think I've ever been to this school or seen your cannery here. I'd love to know more about that."

"I don't know as much as I should about our cannery," Laura said, noticing the way Evan perked up. Connor still stared at his phone, or at least he pretended to. "It's been in operation for more than fifty years. From what I understand, people from miles away used to come here to put up their harvests of vegetables, fruit, even meat. But it's been in decline for a while now."

Anne nodded slowly, with an odd light in her green eyes. She didn't look like she was being polite or that she was surprised or disappointed that the cannery wasn't doing well.

Anne Griffith looked like she'd found a *mission*.

She took Evan's hand.

"That might go very well with what you're teaching, Evan. What you might want to teach here. Maybe we should drop in and introduce ourselves. Anyone you'd recommend we speak with, Laura?"

Laura blinked, trying to get her thoughts moving in a different direction.

She'd expected to be talking to Evan about teaching, and to Anne about getting involved with the high school and the community as well. Her decades of work as a librarian in a huge university library system were every bit as rare and valuable in a small town as a history professor's. Probably even more so.

Noticing the cooking apple smell was the first time Laura had thought of the cannery since…well, since she'd been in high school here herself.

"I'd suggest Linda Burns. She teaches sort of a home economics class, works with the Future Farmers of America, the 4-H club, things like that. I remember her talking about having classes over at the cannery whenever she had enough interest. And enough funding. I'd imagine you have research skills Linda will be thrilled to learn more about, Anne."

Anne nodded, again like she'd known exactly what Laura was going to say. It was less creepy than strangely comforting.

"We'll walk over there, then," she said, then she winked at Laura. "Don't worry, we'll be fine. We've got your contact information and you have ours. I'm certain we'll be in touch."

Evan put his arm around Anne and smiled.

"Maybe you can talk to Connor a bit, Laura. He hasn't been to Wolf Branch for a few years. I'm sure he'd like to know more about where we're living now."

And they turned and walked away.

Laura took a deep breath, determined to be pleasant, no matter how hard that might be with an annoying guy. Still cute, absolutely. Not to mention easily distracted and not even aware that his parents were walking off on their own.

He seemed like the type that would wander off, maybe right into traffic, fussing with his digital nanny. She'd probably have to track him down right now.

She turned and nearly crashed right into Connor.

"I'm sorry," he said, his eyes wide and stricken. "I didn't expect you to… I didn't mean to startle you."

"I'm fine, nothing to worry about. I was going to speak to you, anyway."

He tilted his head to the side, and the setting sun caught the green in his eyes.

Laura forced herself to ignore that. Or at least she tried.

"Your parents are off to the cannery to introduce themselves. I think that could be a nice fit with your mother's research expertise and your father's teaching. Any questions I can answer for you about Wolf Branch?"

Connor drew back, looking startled himself. He glanced toward the cannery just in time to see his parents go through the double glass doors.

"I wouldn't even know where to start. We drove around the whole town today, which didn't take long at all." He shook his head and scowled before Laura could say a word. "No, I'm sorry, that's not how I meant it. It seems like a nice town."

"It is, thank you." Laura forced herself to smile, hoping it was somewhere in the neighborhood of natural. "Tell me about yourself, then. What do you do up there in Chicago?"

He shrugged, looking down and kicking at the cracked pavement under his feet.

"My bachelor's degree is in architecture, and the plan has always been that I'd get a master's in that, too."

"The plan? You have your own planners? *Please* tell me how to get that set up for myself."

He looked up at her under his eyebrows, flashing a shy smile that sent a jolt of warmth through her belly.

"Well, *my* plan. Mom and Dad aren't much help there, really. They just say they want me to be happy. Sometimes I almost envy my friends who had their path laid out by their parents before they ever graduated high school, and enforced all the way through college. Almost."

Laura crossed her arms, surprised and somehow pleased that he'd said so much. She never would have admitted so much personal stuff to someone she just met.

In fact, a whole lot of people she was very close to—including her own parents and Jim—had no idea how…*ambivalent* she felt about her own career path with her freshly minted degree in economics.

"So what path do *you* want, Connor?"

He looked away, this time toward the steep, curving road that led down into Wolf Branch. Hardly anyone was driving up here, but she could see and hear what passed for rush hour in town.

"I don't know," he said, then shook his head and met her gaze again. "Yeah, I do know. I've been putting off grad school for three years now, claiming I want to save up for it or get ready or whatever my excuse of the day is. My jobs for supposedly saving up and getting ready have been working with building crews. Houses, schools, churches, hospitals. Anyone who would take me on, basically."

He took a deep breath, and she noticed how his broad shoulders stayed tense when it let if out. As if she was going to yell and scream at him, or worse yet, say she was so *very* disappointed in him.

She wished she didn't recognize his feelings quite so well.

She waved one hand toward the track.

"Go for a walk with me? If your parents met up with Linda, they'll be quite a while."

"Sure. All those hours in the car were brutal to say the

least. And if Mom and Dad really get going, a while might turn into a few hours."

They headed toward the path, both of them adjusting their pace to get into the empty space between the other walkers.

"The hard truth," he finally said, "at least hard for people who don't live in my head, is I like the building a hell of a lot better than the designing." He shook his head and pressed his lips together, and Laura couldn't help noticing now nicely they were shaped. He spoke so quickly she had to strain to understand. "I just don't think I really want to be an architect any more."

She tried her best, but she couldn't stop herself from smiling. Connor raised his eyebrows.

"No, I'm sorry," she said. "I'm not glad you're having trouble or want to make a change or anything like that. It's just…you remind me of me. Have you said that out loud to anyone else?"

"Have I…" They took several paces, their strides quick and coordinated, before he went on. "Well, no. Not until just now, as a matter of fact. I have to admit I'm a little surprised I managed."

"Want to say it again? Don't laugh, I'm serious. Listen, I'll go first. I haven't said this out loud yet either." She took a deep breath, amazed at how hard the words fought her efforts to push them out into the open air. "I, Laura Michaelson, do *not* want to become any sort of institutional or big government economist."

Chapter 4

AFTER HER DECLARATION, almost as shaky and fast as his own, Laura let her breath out in a *whoosh*. Connor grinned.

"Let me guess. You have a shiny new degree in economics. It was all kinds of fun to study, but once you started thinking about what you'd actually do with that degree, all the fun went away."

"Got it in one," she said. "I loved learning the theory, the way all the systems fit together and feed off each other for better and for worse. The ways economies rise or fall, sometimes for reasons that would be totally irrational unless you consider that humans are involved. But the idea of doing the *work,* especially for government or big cities. Or even teaching. The research, the meetings, having your findings ignored over and over again. I feel like I'm drowning just thinking about it."

They'd made it to the far side of the football field, right alongside all those gorgeous trees. Connor couldn't pretend to himself that Laura didn't outshine them all.

"I wish I didn't understand so well," he said. "Even before I finished up, I was getting envious of the people I saw doing the building. Making something change every day, creating something that would last. It sounds hokey, I know, but using their hands, working outside. Once I took the first summer job after I graduated, it was all over."

"I feel the same way about working with the town and the school. I'm working with numbers, sure. And forecasting a bit, and budgeting, and explaining what I find. But people actually listen, and not years later, either. I see good things happening here *now* because of what I can do."

He looked at her again, then almost wished he hadn't.

The way she bit her lip…

"Getting flak from your folks?"

She held out her left hand and tilted it back and forth. Her fingers were slender, delicate, and ring-free.

"A little, not bad. More from my grandparents. I didn't expect *them* to be pushing me to move away of all things. Wanting me to run off to the big city. Aren't they supposed to be the ones hounding us to come home and visit every time we turn around?"

Connor laughed under his breath, not quite willing to get into discussing *his* grandparents. Not even after he'd laid all his complicated feelings about his career on the line with a woman he'd only met less than half an hour ago.

His mother's parents were sweet and loving, even if his Grandmother Fincastle seemed perpetually amazed by his existence, even after twenty-five years.

His father's father was always warm and friendly and great fun when Connor was a kid.

But as he'd gotten older, he'd understood why his dad and his Auntie Gwen sometimes referred to their father as Hurricane Ed. The moody and snappish and somehow unnerving aspects of his personality were invisible, or maybe hidden, around Ed's young grandkids and now his great-grandkids.

Anyone who was in their late teen years or beyond invariably caught them, like a warning scent of a wildfire drifting on the wind.

"So if you're not getting trouble from your parents," Laura said, apparently picking up on Connor's unease, "who's pushing you? Besides yourself, which I totally understand."

"That's easy," he said, even though saying it out loud to Laura very much was not. "Trish. My…well, I suppose she's my girlfriend. She's studying law, and I think she'd prefer I got on with it and jumped on the appropriate career ladder with her."

He glanced at Laura quickly enough to catch her sad smile, then realized a beat later that he'd misunderstood it. Her response had nothing to do with him mentioning Trish at all.

"Yeah, there is that. My boyfriend Jim is exactly the same way. He's one semester away from his bachelors in political science, planning to go to UVA and take me with him so we can both go for our doctorates. Which to him and my grandparents is the only thing that makes sense, so why discuss it? Never mind that I don't particularly want *any* of that."

"I'm going to take a guess based on how it's been going for me," Connor said. "No one's asking you that simple question, but I will. What *do* you want, Laura?"

This time her smile was sweet and grateful.

"You're right about no one asking. Thank you. The pathetic answer is I'm not sure. Wanting to stay right here in this same small town feels…strange. But maybe not as strange as disappearing into a life that doesn't quite fit. Now, fair's fair. What do *you* want, Connor? To work as a general contractor or something like that?"

"Well yeah, maybe. That might make sense someday. Once I get a lot more experience. Sure. I'd have to learn the fine art of budgeting and estimates and such for that, huh?"

Laura nodded, her face serious, but her wonderful eyes twinkled.

"You would indeed need to learn that. Might have to find a friendly economist for coaching while you study. Maybe one who'd be happy to learn about a new field herself."

"I'll keep that advice in mind," Connor said, trying his best to keep his grin to himself. "And I'll be sure to ask you for references when the time comes."

They'd made it back around to the cannery, just in time to see Connor's parents walk out with a woman he didn't recognize. She was younger than them, not much older than him, with brown hair piled in a sloppy bun on top of her head.

"There's Linda," Laura said, slowing her pace and heading for the gate. Connor couldn't think of anything else to do but follow her. "If your folks want to help out at the cannery or the high school, they're in the best possible hands."

"I'm sure they'll be fine. I think this will be a good change for them."

Laura stopped with her hands on her hips, staring at him. Connor struggled not to fidget or look away.

"I have to apologize to you, Connor. I really did mean to answer any questions you had about Wolf Branch. All we did was complain about our own lives. Promise you'll let me know if I can do anything to help?"

Nothing that flashed through his mind needed to make it out of his mouth.

Keep walking with me.

Tell me what would make you happy that *doesn't* include this Jim guy.

Talk to me about anything and everything.

Help me deal with the awful guilt about thinking all these things about you when I really should call Trish.

"Sometimes venting is good for the soul," he said. "No need to apologize. I hope I'll see you again before I leave?"

She nodded once with a big smile.

"I hope so too. And thanks for listening."

He watched as she walked over to his parents and Linda, speaking to all of them and shaking hands before she headed toward the few remaining cars.

"Calling Trish," he said under his breath. "Remember? Trish? Your…girlfriend, or whatever this is?"

His voice dropped to a whisper.

"I, Connor Griffith, do *not* want to be an architect. I'd rather build things myself."

Even that sent a shiver of unease through his body, as if Trish could hear him. Or maybe Laura's grandparents.

He held up his hand when she drove past in a tiny little white car and waved at him. An entirely different and not at all unpleasant shiver passed through him then.

Connor shook his head, sighed, and walked back to his parents.

Chapter 5

THE SCREENED-IN back porch at Laura's house normally seemed spacious. Tonight it felt downright crowded and cramped and stuffed full of too many people.

This was one of those times when it felt much more like her parents' house than hers.

The long glass-topped table had seated up to ten people during big family gatherings, with smaller tables for the overflow off to the side, inside, or even out in the level, tree and flower-filled yard. Only four places were set tonight with her mother's fancy pink outdoor dining plates and bowls and cups, with dark green woven placemats underneath and matching napkins with dragonfly napkin rings to complete the overpowering effect.

Sort of like a last desperate effort to hold on to the summer that had already passed them by.

A row of bumblebee lights hung from the ceiling, with black wire wings flung out and bulbs protruding from their yellow and black striped bellies. Laura thought they were cute on a good night. Right now they looked ghastly and silly to her eyes.

The food was reliably fantastic, with her dad's grilling skills and her mom's delight in elaborate side dishes on full display. A spring gazpacho made with fresh herbs and good tomatoes that had to have been hard to find so late in the year to start with. Then skewers full of big, pink shrimp marinated to perfection along with whole-wheat orzo with fresh mint and olive oil, and grilled asparagus covered with toasted almond slivers.

Her mother sat across from Laura, wearing a stubbornly cheery sundress, too, covered with huge daisies in pastel shades. The sunshine yellow sweater she'd pulled on against the autumn chill matched the centers of the daisies perfectly.

She'd tried to convince Laura to dress up for dinner too, saying her boring work uniform of jeans and a button-up was too drab and awful for guests. After a few tense exchanges that were definitely too loud for company, Laura had finally managed to get her to back off.

A reminder that she was twenty-two and had lived away for four years shouldn't have been required to get clearance to make her own clothing choices, no.

But sometimes the battles were worth fighting.

After all, Jim was hardly a rare and terribly important guest for dinner after over two years of dating. It seemed like he was here more often than he was at his own house lately. Laura hadn't expected him at all tonight, and the surprise grated on her somehow.

For one thing, Jim had dressed up, far more than he usually did for…well, anything in Laura's experience. Unlike her father, who'd refused to change out of his normal *I'm at home now* standard of a colorful Hawaiian shirt and casual khaki pants, Jim looked like he was dressed for a flipping job interview of all things.

He sat beside her in long-sleeved midnight blue shirt—but unlike Laura's, this was a straight-up, delicate dress shirt rather than the sturdy work version. He wore a burgundy tie to emphasize the point, which he'd flipped back over his shoulder even though he'd carefully (and pretentiously) tucked one of those green cloth napkins at his throat before eating. Another napkin protected his lap, or more correctly the black dress pants he'd worn for some insane reason.

He'd freshly shaved his handsome, square-jawed face, and combed and controlled his thick black hair within an inch of its life.

With all of Jim's and her mother's obsessive preparation, Laura was more than half tempted to accidently knock the deep red soup into their laps just to see how excited everyone got.

As the three of them small-talked without much participation from her, Laura tried to remember how excited she used to get simply by being around Jim. How they'd seemed like such a perfect match while they were at college, supporting each other, encouraging each other, seeming to know what the other needed without either having to ask.

And she wondered exactly when—and why—that had started to fade.

She shook her head and forced herself to pay attention when she caught her name drifting through the conversational haze.

"I'm sorry," she said, not even sure who'd spoken. "Lost in my thoughts."

Her mother pursed her lips—still perfectly outlined in pink lipstick even after the soup and shrimp.

"I was just wondering how your day went, dear. You had to work later than usual."

Laura smiled, surprised at how much her mood lifted at the thought of the Griffiths.

"Today was good. We worked on the budget to update the hospital, mainly. What we need to bring it more in line with modern standards for disaster recovery. Then I met with a new couple who just moved here from Chicago, really nice people. A history professor and a professional librarian."

Her mother gave the raised-eyebrow nod that meant she was impressed, and her father smiled and leaned forward.

"Hey, that's wonderful," he said. "I'd like to meet them myself."

Jim, on the other hand, snorted and shook his head.

"Why on earth did they come to Wolf Branch, of all places? Even if they wanted to get out of Chicago, there had to be somewhere with more going on than here."

Laura's mother didn't even glance in Jim's direction or seem to hear, but her father shot a quick and unnoticed scowl his way.

Laura herself was immediately furious. All at once, she'd had *more* than enough of Jim's utter lack of interest in the important work she was doing, and his growing distaste for their hometown.

Never mind that she'd thought almost exactly the same thing while she waited for the Griffiths a few hours ago.

"I'd be happy to introduce you, Mom and Dad." Laura turned up her bright, cheerful voice and leaned away from Jim. "They sure are interesting, and very friendly. Maybe we could have them over for lunch or dinner before it really does get too cold outside. They talked to Linda Burns at the cannery, too. I hope they can work together to bring it back to life a little bit. If we invite Linda, she might be able to bring some of the applesauce or apple butter I smelled cooking today."

Her father raised one eyebrow a tiny bit, obviously aware of how Laura was feeling.

Her mother seemed to miss it altogether.

"Yes, let's *do* that," she said. "Tomorrow night if you can arrange it. Linda's more than welcome, of course. So that will be seven altogether, then."

Laura took a deep breath, not sure if she was willing to say what she was thinking out loud. A long, frustrated sigh from her left—Jim expressing an opinion he clearly expected to be asked about—settled it for her.

"That's right," she said. "Seven. The Griffiths have their *son* with them." She hoped the dim light hid the flush she felt spreading across her cheeks.

"Is that right?" her father said, now trying to hide his smile. "He's moving here as well?"

"I don't think so," Laura said, still refusing to look at Jim. "He's helping them get settled in. He'll eventually head back to Chicago."

Laura's mother opened her mouth, then closed it. She was very much on Team Jim, while tonight wasn't the first time Laura's father had picked up on their cooling relationship.

"Well, he's most certainly welcome," her mother said, flashing a quick glance at Jim. "What's his name? What does he do?"

"His name is Connor. He's…he has a degree in architecture. Right now he's working on the building side instead of design, thinking about going back for a master's."

She flushed a bit more at her words, when she knew very well that Connor had no intention of continuing his education, at least not in architecture.

Not any more than Laura herself intended to go for a doctorate in economics.

"Well *good* for him," Jim said a bit too loudly, apparently tired of not being part of the conversation. "Getting an advanced degree makes *good* sense in that field. He'll find better programs up there, some of the best. Much like

Virginia has the best political science programs. Economics, too."

Something in his voice finally got Laura to look at him, and the firm set of his mouth and jaw confirmed it. Jim was jealous, or at least worried, about a guy he'd never even heard of two minutes ago. A strange expression that sat very uncomfortably on his face.

Maybe he'd noticed the coolness between them after all.

"I'll look forward to hearing more about that," her father said, now smiling openly. "Maybe Connor could give you and the town some advice on the renovations at the hospital."

Laura nodded, smiling back at him. "That's a great idea, Dad. He knows both the design and the work side of things now, so that can't hurt. He mentioned hospitals specifically. I'll ask him about that tomorrow."

"That's settled, then," Laura's mother said, folding her hands on the table in front of her. "Do you mind to help me take a few of these things inside, Laura? Then we'll bring out dessert. Maybe you and Jim can take a walk while you eat."

She stood and picked up a plate full of abandoned shrimp skewers and the empty soup bowl and went through the open sliding glass door before Laura could answer. She started to gather up her plate and Jim's, but he touched her arm.

"I'll get these together," he said close to her ear. "Then we really should take that walk."

Laura turned and studied him. From his slight smile to his dainty ears to the scattering of freckles across his nose, he looked a whole lot like the guy she'd met years ago in high school right here in town. The guy she'd struck up a casual friendship with while they both pursued other people, but they never quite got around to dating each other.

"Thank you, Jim," she said, picking up plates with the

remains of the orzo and asparagus and heading into the house.

She and Jim hadn't started dating even after they both went to the same college a few hours away, though they did stay friends. She could pinpoint the moment things changed between them, even if she never had quite understood why.

A recruitment event for graduate schools, back when Laura was a junior and still intrigued by that idea. She and Jim had sat side by side, whispering their snarky or excited responses to each other the whole time.

By the end of the presentations and the meet-and-greet and the mingling, they were holding hands.

By the end of the semester, everyone considered them as good as engaged, without either of them ever saying yes or no. People hardly bothered to ask.

That bugged Laura a little bit in the beginning, but she and Jim were having fun, so she'd ignored it. Same as she hadn't bothered to say a word to anyone when the two of them started to drift apart after she graduated.

When she saw the look in her mother's eyes, the way she stood in the middle of the kitchen with her head up and hands on her hips, Laura realized she might have made a mistake on both parts.

"What do you mean, talking like that, excluding Jim when he's sitting right there beside you?"

Laura walked past and scraped the plates into the garbage, then dropped them into the dishwasher. Like everything else in the kitchen, the dishwasher was matte tan, nowhere near as bright as the summertime dishes. Easier to keep clean, and coordinate all the different seasonal and special occasion curtains and pot holders and everything else with, don't you know.

"I don't recall anyone inviting Jim to dinner tomorrow

night," Laura said, taking a few steps back toward the door. "Or asking me if he could come to dinner tonight."

"Since when do we have to *ask* who we invite to dinner? Jim has practically been a member of this family for two years now."

Laura's determination to avoid a fight slipped. She crossed her arms and stared back at her mother.

"I never said he was a member of the family, Mom. Last time I checked that was still up to me. We've just been *dating*, for goodness sake. No rings have exchanged hands. I don't expect them to, either."

Her mother narrowed her eyes and took a deep breath.

Laura's full stomach twisted itself into a knot.

The unannounced dinner. Jim's fancy clothes. Her mother trying to get her to dress up, too.

No. Oh no.

Please don't say it.

Please don't be *true*.

"At the rate you're going tonight, the exchange of rings is getting less likely by the minute."

Laura walked out before her mother could say another word.

Her father met her by the sliding glass door, his hands full of the rest of the dishes.

"I got this, hon. Why don't you and Jim go ahead and take that walk? He's in the yard."

She scowled, wondering when her dad had decided to switch sides. He shook his head and leaned in to give her a quick kiss on the cheek.

"I'm not pushing you toward anything you're not ready for, you know that. Might be good to clear the air no matter what's going on, you know?"

"Yeah, I know. Thanks, Dad." She kissed his cheek, then went out the screen door to look for Jim.

Chapter 6

Though he felt a bit guilty about it after talking to Laura, Connor fully expected the restaurant situation in Wolf Branch to be dire. In fact, he'd planned on avoiding it altogether, hoping a short visit full of helping his parents would give him the perfect excuse.

Sorry, too busy getting the house organized. You two go on without me.

Unfortunately for those plans, the house had come together in record time. With two excited local kids helping, the whole house had been sorted and arranged that afternoon.

His parents had packed everything perfectly. Everything except the loads of books they'd brought with them in numbered boxes according to which built-in shelf they belonged on. Shelves that had been planned, but were so far nothing more than piles of lumber and nails and screws on the back porch.

Everyone, including Connor, agreed he'd be the best one to measure and build those shelves to perfection.

Now he sat with his parents and Linda Burns in a

surprisingly pleasant hotel restaurant, eating an absurdly good appetizer of tangy sourdough bread, fresh butter, and local apple butter cooked down to almost brick red perfection. According to Linda, that was the fantastic aroma outside the cannery earlier.

Connor couldn't help closing his eyes in pleasure with every bite he took.

The place itself was much nicer than he imagined he'd find hours away from the nearest city. A gleaming pale hardwood floor made with broad strips of recycled wood. Elaborately patterned tin ceilings over a hundred years old, and as nice as anything he'd ever seen in Chicago. Purposely mismatched place settings and salt and pepper shakers that somehow managed to be charming.

And a fully stocked bar with a bartender who looked like a local lumberjack with red hair and a burly beard, but he made the best martini Connor had ever tasted.

Turned out Linda was more than happy to have all the help she could get with the cannery and the high school, and she'd already arranged a meeting with the town library the next morning.

Connor had never managed to fit in anywhere as well as his parents already did in Wolf Branch.

Linda was already a bit red-cheeked from her own glass of wine, and her carefully braided hair had somehow managed to dis-arrange itself. But her passion and excitement were contagious enough to keep the conversation going.

"You didn't mention pollinators this afternoon," she said, mock-glaring at his father. "I've been wanting to set up hives somewhere near the high school for years now. These kids don't appreciate how close we came to losing them all not that long ago."

Connor wasn't surprised to see his dad glance at his mom before answering. Connor didn't mind one way or the other, but his mom had a deep and abiding fear of honeybees in particular. All he knew was she'd had too many nightmares about them.

"I've never had a good space in the city to set up hives," his dad said. "I was hoping to keep a few at home. I'd love to get some hands-on experience."

Connor's mother shivered. "I'll take a pass on that, thank you very much, even though I know they're great for gardens. Have you thought about setting up a community garden? To go with the cannery?"

When his phone buzzed in his pocket, Connor only felt a slight twinge of guilt. The conversation was going just fine without him.

Still at dinner?

Trish, of course. He hadn't much wanted to chat with her earlier, but now he was grateful for the interruption.

Yeah. They're down to business talk now, deep into the honeybees and hive takeover planning.

A tiny, eerie likeness of her flashed across his screen, like a slightly unnatural computer-enhanced version of a long-dead actress, throwing her brown hair back and laughing. Connor knew she'd recorded the avatars to match whatever response she wanted. He'd seen her make some of them, trying over and over again to get it just right.

The effect still unnerved him.

Restaurant as horrid as you expected?

Connor glanced at his parents and Linda, then grabbed the last palm-sized bit of sourdough bread. He dragged it through the remains of the apple butter and popped it into his mouth.

Quite good, actually. Visits down here won't be nearly as deprived as I thought.

Except I won't be with you. And you WILL miss me.

Odd and slightly annoying as he found all the little

custom avatars, he couldn't help smiling at her lips making a personalized kissing motion, followed by a close-up of her exaggerated flirty eyes blinking.

I miss you already. You'd love it here, might want to join me for a visit sometime.

As soon as he hit Send, a vision of Laura's hair glowing in the sunset flashed up in Connor's mind. The idea of Trish down here sneering and making snide little remarks about everything grated on his nerves.

The two of them doing the same thing together just a few days ago felt totally different after the pride he'd so clearly seen in Laura's eyes.

Well, for a visit, maybe. You need to get back up here to the city. And me.

This time the tiny figure actually raised her shirt and flashed. Despite the cartoon aspect, Connor blushed and looked up.

Right into his mother's eyes.

"Got something distracting you, son?"

He knew he was blushing more than enough to bother lying.

"Yes, I'm sorry. Let me step outside to take this."

He hadn't lived with his parents full-time for more than five years, but he still paused, waiting for some sort of permission. When his mother finally nodded once, he excused himself and escaped into the cool night air, fragrant with wood smoke from somewhere nearby.

The restaurant had a broad lawn behind it with a small stage, fire pit, and chairs scattered around. Thankfully only a few people sat close to the fire. Connor walked away toward the sidewalk and thumbed the icon to switch from chat to call.

"That was quick," Trish said, laughter obvious in her voice.

"I had to get out of there. I could hardly ogle you in front of my parents. Not even cartoon style."

"What can I say? I'm bored and lonely without you."

Connor shook his head and turned left at the sidewalk, toward the main street and its rows of brick buildings. A few other people were out walking around under the rows of black streetlights that looked like old gas versions, but he had privacy enough.

Trish hadn't seemed this interested in him for anything besides sex for a long while now. And, well, he'd been feeling about the same way.

"I won't be down here forever," he said. "A couple of weeks at most."

"I know, and I'm swamped with studying anyway. I guess I didn't expect to miss you quite this much."

Connor smiled as he took another left to walk in front of the restaurant's big windows. His parents and Linda were still deep in conversation, and doing perfectly fine without him. Like he'd expected Trish to do back in Chicago.

"I'm glad to hear you like having me around," he said. "We'll have to do something about that as soon as I get back."

She laughed, and he wondered what sort of animation she would have sent in a text. He wasn't quite bold enough to switch to a video call right there on the street.

"You never know what surprises I have planned for you. Better get back to your folks before you get in trouble."

"I think it's too late for that already. I'll call you when I get up tomorrow."

"Are you really going to tell me you're not up right now, Connor? Not even a little bit?"

Connor rubbed his mouth and smiled, leaning back against the brick wall of the restaurant.

"You got me there, Trish."

"If I was down there with you, I'd have you for damn sure. Sweet dreams."

She ended the call, leaving Connor staring at the phone and shaking his head. He couldn't manage to call what he had with Trish love, no matter how hard he might try to convince himself. Nothing like what his parents had.

But what he had with her wasn't half bad.

Maybe getting back to Chicago sooner than later wouldn't be so bad, either.

Chapter 7

THE HUGE BACK yard was full of various shapes and sizes of flower beds, bushes, and garden beds that her mother adored, and surrounded by perfectly trimmed grass that Laura's father took great pride in. All of it already cleaned up for autumn despite the summer-themed dinner.

Knee-high solar lights shaped like dragonflies, humming-birds, and her mother's favorite bumblebees reflected off of newly planted bunches of mums in all colors. Bunches of cheerful yellow black-eyed Susans, speckled toad lilies, dainty pale blue asters, and neatly tended roses and other flowers ready for hibernation decorated the path.

The garden beds still held winter squash growing fat and happy on trellises, wrinkly dark green kale like miniature forests, and thatches of smooth collard greens that tasted bitter to Laura no matter how they were cooked.

Her father had laid down a winding path through the whole thing a couple of years ago made of shredded tires dyed dark brown. Laura slowly followed it, and found Jim exactly where she'd expected him.

Sitting on the covered wooden swing toward the back,

with three hearts carved into the back of the seat. Right in the middle, too, so Laura would have to sit close to him.

To be fair, that's exactly where she'd wanted to sit until not so very long ago.

"Care to join me?" he said, his smile clear by the soft glow of multi-colored fairy lights strung across the arched wooden top of the swing.

Laura couldn't help smiling back, remembering the first time she'd brought him here after they'd started dating. Her parents were openly affectionate enough to be slightly embarrassing when company wasn't around, so she couldn't pretend she and Jim were the first to make love on the swing.

The memory was one of her favorites with him or anyone else she'd ever dated.

"Be glad to," she said.

He scooted to one side without her saying a word.

She never could resist pushing off to start the swing, and her mood lightened with the gentle motion.

"So what's going on in your head today?" he said, same as they'd both always done in high school. "By the way, I can't make dinner tomorrow night anyway."

Laura smiled and reached over and took his hand, enjoying the warmth against the cool night air.

"Thank you. It's a big old mess inside my head today," she said. "Nothing new there. How about you?"

He shrugged, then took his turn pushing off with his feet. Laura noticed he wore dress shoes, too, black and pointy-toed. She couldn't remember the last time she'd seen him dressed like this outside of church or a formal dance, or an actual job interview.

"Full of school stuff mostly. Thinking about graduating, what comes next."

"Did you talk to a recruiter today? Or something equally formal?"

He laughed, shaking his head. His voice was sad enough when he spoke to bring tears to Laura's eyes.

"Nothing like that. Just seemed like a good idea at the time."

Laura tried not to get anxious again, or panic about what his next words might be.

It wasn't that she was truly horrified at the idea of Jim proposing to her. She'd thought about it more than once. For a while there about a year ago, she'd been hoping for it, expecting it. The trouble was more that she didn't want to hurt his feelings, or make him feel stupid if her reaction showed how she really felt.

Even if she hadn't enjoyed talking to Connor so much, and wanted to talk to him a lot more, she couldn't imagine spending her life with someone who just didn't seem to…*match* with her any more.

"Well, you look nice," she said. "UVA or any other school would be lucky to have you."

"What about you?"

Her mind raced, thinking of more ways to interpret his words than could possibly be good for her. She decided on the least scary option.

"I'm not so sure any grad school wants someone like me. Not right now. Those seats would be better filled with someone who really wants to be there, don't you think?"

Jim nodded silently and pushed the swing back again.

"I've been thinking a lot about that, Laura. And looking into places to live in Charlottesville that don't care if you're in school or not. Places to work, too."

She watched his face, wishing the light were brighter so she could get an idea how he was feeling. That was the first time he'd ever mentioned anything besides her going to school with him, *being* in school herself.

Much as she was beginning to enjoy her work and her

place in Wolf Branch, a move to a bigger city without the pressure to go back to school didn't sound all that bad.

"Have you decided when you're going?" she said. "January or May?"

He shrugged again, squeezing her hand a little.

"They have space for me either time. I don't have to say for a couple of weeks yet. I thought I might leave that up to you."

Laura stared up at the lights, wishing clouds weren't blocking out the stars. She wanted to look at something unchanging, at least compared to the whiplash of her thoughts and feelings.

"You're willing to let me think about it? And no pushing me about school?"

Jim kicked them back a little too hard, setting up a sideways twist instead of a smooth swing.

"I won't lie to you," he said. "I don't understand why you don't want to go back. You're so smart and so good at what you're doing now. You could do loads more with another degree. And…that's the last thing I'll say about it."

"The last thing? Promise?"

He took a deep breath and looked at her, and Laura could see he was smiling. She still couldn't quite see his eyes.

"I promise. You're worth it, Laura. You're worth that and so much more."

Laura closed her eyes, trying to catch hold of how she felt about that.

And she couldn't.

But she appreciated him more than she could say for trying.

"Thank you, Jim. Truly. Can I have a week to think about it?"

He leaned toward her, and she felt a distant echo of their original heat when their lips met.

"You can have two. More if you need it."

Laura scooted over to meet him in the middle, her head fitting his shoulder as well as always. She pushed the swing back into a gentle glide, with only a hint of the odd pattern.

And she wondered why she kept seeing Connor's green eyes and his shy smile.

Chapter 8

Even after a full morning and afternoon of work, the library-in-progress didn't look like much. Red chalk lines snapped on the tan walls worked like reverse ghosts. Marking not where shelves had been for years on end, but where they would be before the end of the day, and for years to come.

Widely spaced on the bottom, carefully measured to hold tall books full of photographs. The boards would be wide, too, creating enough room for the huge-format volumes to fit comfortably. Smaller toward the middle, then close together and narrow for the last few at the top. Perfect for row upon row of battered paperbacks from long before Connor was born.

The final space near the ceiling still looked too tall to his eyes, even though he knew it would be jammed full of photographs. Lovingly framed and often containing evidence of his own awkward childhood.

The living room visible through the arched entryway already looked amazingly like home to Connor's eyes. Most of the furniture he knew so well from his parents' apartment fit perfectly into the cozy space. It might have all been bought for here rather than packed up and hauled hundreds of miles.

The house already smelled the same too, with lingering scents of coffee and his mother's cinnamon ginger cookies floating through the air.

Making sure the rather *less* pleasant aroma of quick-drying wood stain didn't linger just as strongly in the air was exactly why Connor and his father worked the wood out in the big, mostly flat back yard. Measuring, sawing, sanding, and now staining the amazing number of shelves of all sizes needed to hold the mountains of books still packed up in boxes in the guest bedroom, leaving him barely enough room to walk through.

In fact, Connor had been inside measuring long enough, letting his dad do the grunt work. He'd just finished getting a door going into the hallway partly covered over, ready to hold more shelves and books rather than an opening they didn't need. He headed through the kitchen and met his mother coming in from outside.

"How's he doing out there?" Connor said.

His mom smiled. "He's happy as a clam. Finally in his own backyard, with plenty of room to putter. Fair warning, he's already got a long list of projects in mind for you."

"I better get busy then."

"Hang on, I think he'll be just fine," his mom said, handing him a spring green mug full of hot apple cider and two crispy brown cookies still warm from the oven on a matching plate. "You're going to run off up north soon enough. Sit down in here with me for a minute."

Connor glanced around the kitchen, automatically looking to catalog anything that needed to be done before he left.

A surprising number of cabinets lined the walls in the small space, nearly as many as they'd had in a bigger kitchen in Chicago. Flowery linoleum and bright yellow walls added a cheery touch. The familiar row of colorful cookbooks already tucked onto a shelf along with the shiny red stand mixer and matching blender he'd grown up with turned it into home.

His mother waited at a small oak table in the corner, one of the few new purchases they'd made for the move. The sturdy tan square could add leaves for company, but it would mostly be for two.

"Everything looks like it's been here for years," he said, sitting across from her. "Except for the library. That's a dusty mess."

"That will come together soon enough. Linda sent this cider, it's wonderful."

Connor took a sip, sighing at the tart sweetness. He nibbled an edge off a cookie, adding spicy heat to the mix.

"Perfect for the cookies. I'm going to miss these when I go home."

She shook her head and rolled her eyes.

"As if you hadn't helped me make them about a thousand times. And I hadn't printed out that recipe and a whole bunch more."

"Well, they won't be quite the same. What can I do besides the shelves so we can get all those boxes of books off the front porch?"

"You're doing plenty, son, just helping us out. *We* won't be quite the same without seeing you more than a couple of times a year."

Connor tried to find the words to argue, to say he'd be down here a lot more than that. But not to say it without making a promise he was afraid he'd end up breaking no matter what his intentions were right that second.

"I'll visit as often as I can. I really do like it here, more than I thought I would. Beautiful town. This house is nice and private. Nice people around here, too."

His mom lifted her eyebrow for a split second, so fast he wasn't even sure he'd seen it.

"That reminds me, I had a call from that lovely young woman who met us yesterday. What was her name?"

"Laura," Connor said a little bit too fast. "Laura Michaelson. She called?"

"She did. Said her parents would love to have us over for dinner tonight. Sort of a welcome to town. You're certainly welcome to join us unless you have other plans."

Connor drank a bit more of his cider, using the excuse to avoid his mom's eyes.

"I wouldn't want to intrude, especially since I'm going back soon. Did Laura invite just you two, or all of us?"

Again that fleeting eyebrow raise.

"If I'm remembering correctly, she said me, Evan, and you. All three of us *and* individually. Might not be so bad to have a few friends down here for when you do visit."

"Might not."

Connor tried to ignore the images of Laura floating through his mind. Smiling, laughing, walking by his side yesterday. For some odd reason, those were more clear than the tiny little cartoon character Trish had sent to long-distance flash him.

"I know this isn't your favorite subject to discuss," his mom said, watching his face, "but I'm going to ask because video calls won't be the same as talking to you. What are you going to do when you get back?"

He smiled. "You mean about baking cookies?"

She narrowed her eyes and scowled, all of it a light-hearted version of the very real expressions he'd frequently earned as a stubborn teenager.

"Yes, that's *exactly* what I mean. How *ever* will you get

through the rest of your life without me to bake cookies for you? Especially since you haven't lived with us since you were nineteen."

Connor grinned, finished one of his cookies, and chased it with cider. He pushed the crumbs on the plate around with his fingertip, focusing on that instead of looking into his mother's eyes.

"I better enjoy this while it lasts, then," he said. "When I get back home, I'll go back to work. Doing what I've been doing all day here, mainly. Building things. Trying to figure the rest out as I go."

He finally looked up and saw the curious, calm expression he expected. But as they often did, her eyes told the real story.

They weren't as shadowed as when she'd been having particularly bad dreams. During those times, Connor had often woken to the sound of her voice and his dad's in the middle of the night. Then watched the two of them orbit each other the next morning, with his father moving to put himself between her and anything that could hurt her. As if she'd been ill or in a terrible accident.

From what Connor could tell, on bad nights that was pretty much what she went through.

Now his mother's eyes were lighter somehow. More clear. As if she'd passed through a difficult time and stepped into the sunlight and warmth on the other side.

"It suits you," she said, nodding toward the not-quite library. "Building. Making new things. That's when you're happiest."

"Yeah, it does. I am. That's when I feel…I don't know, most useful. When I do the work with my own hands."

She watched his hands for a second, still restlessly moving the crumbs around.

"More then than when you're making the designs for other people to build."

He held his breath for several seconds, then let it out in a long sigh. Along with tension he hadn't realized was building up across his back and shoulders.

"You're right. Are you trying to tell me I don't have to go back to school if I don't want to?"

"No, not at all. I think it's more trying to tell you it's *okay* if you don't want to. As far as we're concerned, anyway. Don't feel like you'll be disappointing me or your father either way. Make sense?"

"Makes all kinds of sense. More than even I knew before yesterday."

She tilted her head to the side with a small smile. He had a strong feeling she knew the answer before she asked.

"What happened yesterday?"

"Laura and I were talking about school yesterday, while you two were meeting with Linda. About how we both…want a different path than people might expect." He paused, determined to speak more calmly than he had walking around the track. "The truth is I don't want to go back to school. I love what I'm doing, building things. That's what I want to do."

His mother nodded slowly with the same small smile.

"A different path for both of you. I agree. That does make all kinds of sense."

They both turned when his father stopped outside the kitchen door, brushing sawdust from his jeans and stomping his feet before he walked in.

"I thought there might be something good in here." He picked up two cookies and joined them at the table. "Got everything stained and ready to go for the library. It's all drying fast with that cool breeze outside."

"We'll have plenty of time to get the shelves up before

dinner, then," Connor said. "Probably can't get the books all done tonight if we're going out."

He didn't miss the way his parents' eyes met the way they so often did, saying volumes to each other without a single word.

"Sounds great to me," his dad said. "Listen, we've got a good bit of wood left over out there. Think you can build shelves on the other side of that door, too? In the hallway? This house is the perfect size for the two of us, but I doubt two book fiends with almost as many photos could ever have enough shelves."

Connor frowned and stepped back into the library, his mind effortlessly turning the series of red lines into the fully completed project. He shifted the image without moving, bringing the other side of the thick wall into focus.

"Sure, that wouldn't be a problem at all," he said. "That old load-bearing wall will make nice, deep shelves there, too. Plenty of room to leave the door in case someone wants to use it again someday, but those shelves will be good for years and years to come."

He was surprised when his dad put an arm around his shoulder and his mom around his waist. They'd walked up behind while he was deep in thought, then embraced him together the same way they always had.

But the sweet gesture choked him up for some reason today.

Maybe he'd miss them more than he yet realized.

"Thank you, Connor," his father said, and he sounded a bit choked up, too. "That would be perfect."

Chapter 9

UNLIKE THE NIGHT BEFORE, Laura was perfectly happy to put a little more effort into her appearance before dinner with Connor and his family.

But not enough so her mother noticed. She knew it was perverse, of course, that desire to hide when she was taking an action that would make her own mother happy. And she wanted to hide it anyway.

She had more time to think about it than she had the night before, anyway. Her mother had banned her from the kitchen after Laura knocked over a colander full of multicolored salad greens fresh out of the garden, muttering about her being jumpy as a june bug.

Nothing more than a quick shower after work, then using a few sparkling clips to hold back the curls around her face and let the rest hang free. A blouse that brought out the blue in her eyes, sure, but with a nice pair of jeans instead of anything as obvious as a skirt.

She considered adding a bit of makeup, mascara and lipstick at the least. A quick brush of blush along her cheeks, maybe. But the idea of having to worry about keeping it looking nice all night long made her feel tense and tired.

Powders had to be reapplied, mascara felt heavy. Lipstick was a nightmare all its own, especially during a meal. She had no idea how her mother managed to keep hers looking so pristine, or how she managed to get such…*sturdy* lipstick off before going to bed.

The main thing was remembering how free and relaxed she'd felt the day before walking and talking to Connor. How she'd felt more like herself than she had in a long time. Not worried about what she was saying, forcing her face into a perfect or flattering expression.

How she'd said more to him than she'd been able to say to anyone else—including herself—about her shifting and changing plans for the future.

Anne and Evan Griffith seemed every bit as comfortable to Laura in the brief time she'd spoken to them as well.

Feeling obligated to do such an *un*comfortable thing as wearing makeup when she hardly ever did made no sense, no matter how she thought about it.

And before she could think about her face or her hair or why she was so worried about a simple dinner, not to mention why she was so relieved her boyfriend of two years *wasn't* going to be there, she walked out to the back porch.

The endless summer theme had vanished overnight.

Now the whole porch celebrated the autumn well in progress. The cushions on the chairs and the loungers on the porch and out in the yard were now a rich, warm orange, with accent pillows either maple red or vivid yellow. All the bowls and plates were shades of the same colors, and even the glasses were orange with etchings of pumpkins and gourds trailing along the sides.

Covered serving dishes—surely steaming hot—that Laura had never seen before carried out the same harvest motif, either in shape, decoration, or color. Candles, too, though some of those were shaped like extra-thick maple leaves dressed up for the season.

The rich, heady scent of her father's special grilled chicken filled the air. She already saw him in her mind. Making the short walk from his big black grill a few feet away from the porch, tucked in under its own miniature roof. A huge, proud smile on his face, bearing the great gift of his perfectly prepared feast.

The biggest surprise was the lights now hanging over the table. Rather than the cute bumblebees, a row of gigantic acorn caps with lights serving as the nut illuminated the rest.

Laura tried to keep her mouth shut, but she was afraid that would annoy her mother even more. When she stepped onto the porch with an armful of light brown cloth napkins embroidered with leaves and nuts and squash, Laura reached for them.

"Everything looks great, Mom. Where did you find all of this?"

Her mother sniffed, but she handed the napkins over. Tonight she wore a burgundy dress trimmed in gleaming copper accents with matching jewelry. Laura had to admit it suited her beautifully.

"I've had a lot of this for years, Laura. You're usually already back at college by the time I bring it out, you know. Some of it I bought new today, like I do every year."

Laura nodded from the other side of the table, where she was arranging two of the napkins at every place setting. One folded in half to the right, one folded into a little tent on the plate. Something Laura had learned to do when she was barely starting school. Then tucking flatware decorated with tiny leaves that she was certain she would have noticed before into place.

Seven place settings, not eight.

"Well, it's all lovely," she said. "What time are they getting here?"

"Any minute now, according to Linda. She's quite taken with the Griffiths. The parents, at any rate. Sounds like she hasn't spoken to the son very much."

Laura shrugged, trying to hide her smile.

"He seemed very nice to me. Coming all the way down here to help them get settled in and all."

Her mother fussed with the new cushions on one of the loungers.

"Yes, that was good of him. Did you say he's in architecture?"

Laura hesitated, not sure what to make of that tone in her mother's voice.

Was that actual, honest curiosity?

"He has a degree in that, yes. Right now he's working as a builder. Houses, office buildings, hospitals. Getting some experience on that side of things."

Her mother looked the place settings over and nudged a couple of forks into a very slightly different position. That was better than deciding to move all of them, as often happened.

"That's good," she said. "Getting experience with what he'll be asking other people to do. Like you are, seeing how small-town government really works."

Laura drew breath to argue, or to at least say she hadn't said she was going back to school at *all*, then she stopped.

Her mother hadn't said that, not this time. Laura had been reacting to snippy comments she'd heard plenty of times, sure, and quite recently. But not this time. She shook her head.

"Yeah, I'm learning all the time, Mom."

Laura's dad poked his head out the sliding glass doors

then, wearing his normal Hawaiian shirt, this one bright blue with orange and pink hibiscus blooms all over it.

"They just pulled up out front. Want me to toast the bread on the grill, hon? The chicken is ready."

"Smells wonderful," Laura said, smiling at him. "What can I do to help?"

Her parents looked at each other, and she swore a tiny little flash of a smile passed between them. Her dad ducked back inside.

"We've both got a few more things to get ready," her mother said, walking toward the door. "Why don't you stay out here and talk to our guests while we're doing that?"

Laura started to protest, but her mother had already gone into the house. She heard voices raised in greeting and moving toward her.

Her sudden rush of nervousness made no sense at all, but it was real all the same. She felt her cheeks heating, her heart speeding up. And rather than pleasantly cool, the porch felt overly warm all of a sudden.

Part of her job was greeting people, meeting with people, talking to them about what the town needed and what it had to offer. Was this all that different?

When Connor stepped out onto the porch and smiled his shy smile, the slow loop inside Laura's belly told her *yes*.

This was different.

And she might be in big trouble here.

Chapter 10

Connor tried to smile, but not too big or creepy, while doing everything he could not to trip over his own fool feet walking out onto the very nice porch at the Michaelson's house. All while a swarm of seagulls or something equally huge and boisterous were playing tag somewhere between his heart and his stomach.

He tried to focus on that feeling like he'd stepped into a home goods showroom for one thing, rather than on how unbelievably gorgeous Laura was standing there smiling at him.

The color-coordinated lights and tablecloth and plates and bowls and cushions, and all the covered dishes shaped like acorns and gourds and little fall leaf candles felt homey, sure. Almost as if homey meant how the demo unit in a new apartment complex or subdivision might look, but not quite.

The way Laura's blue eyes sparkled, though, and how her hair fell loose and free, just like he'd imagined it would look the night before. That was what demanded every bit of his attention.

"Hey Laura," he managed to say, probably grinning like a dipshit. "Wow, something smells fantastic out here."

She tilted her head to the side. "That's Dad's chicken, about ready to come in off the grill. Come on out, everyone, and find yourself a seat."

Connor realized he'd stopped just one step past the sliding glass door, creating a throat-clearing and feet-shifting traffic jam behind him. Not a damn thing to do about that but blush, mutter an apology, and walk around the table so his parents and Linda could join them on the porch.

He turned toward Laura, who had a lovely pink flush across her own cheeks now, but she managed to smile just fine without looking threatening or silly. And who looked *fantastic* with a soft blue shirt and jeans that hugged her curves just right.

"Good to see you again, Laura," Linda said from right behind Connor. "Looks great out here, Patty."

He turned to see a woman who had to be Laura's mother —but who looked entirely different—step through the door carrying a big tray shaped like a flat pumpkin. She was taller, with darker hair arranged neat and smooth, almost like a wig. Her dress seemed more like she was going to church than a family dinner, too.

She smiled, but the way she looked Connor up and down made him feel uneasy.

"Thank you, Linda. You know how much fun I have with all these arrangements. Keeps me in practice for my decorating clients."

Connor wrestled with his reflex of wanting to help with the tray and his fear that he'd either offend Laura's mother or drop it all over the floor. When he met Laura's gaze, she gave a barely perceptible shake of her head.

Linda put one hand on Connor's shoulder and the other

on his mother's. Linda's barely wrangled hair was quite a contrast to Patty's smooth waves.

"Patty Michaelson," Linda said, "this is Anne and Evan Griffith and their son Connor. Patty's husband Rick should be rattling around out here somewhere."

A deep voice drifted out through the door, and a second later a man walked out carrying a strangely plain wooden tray stacked up with thick slices of whole grain toast. His hair and face and eyes looked so much like Laura that Connor couldn't help smiling.

"I'm here," he said. "Let me get these on the grill and get the chicken brought in, and I'll come right back and say howdy." He paused at the screen door and mock-glared over his shoulder. "Sit, sit! Converse! We'll get you stuffed silly soon enough."

Connor tried to glance around without anyone noticing, doing his best to scope out where he could sit versus where he wanted to sit as everyone shuffled around.

Seven place settings, with one at the head so no one would be abandoned. He noticed then that Laura's father had put down a clear glass with colorful etchings of leaves right in the middle of the plate as he walked by. Empty, yes, but a clear sign of where he intended to sit.

Should Connor sit next to Laura? Across from her? What he wanted to do and what he *should* do with Trish in mind weren't getting along very well at all.

He glanced at Laura, and her eyes were equally wide and stricken.

That's right, *seven*. The Boyfriend Jim was nowhere in evidence this evening. Connor had no idea whether he should be glad or dismayed that the whole thing seemed to bother her as well.

He spotted his parents rolling their eyes at each other, and his mom headed around the table to sit beside him while his Dad scooted one space to the side. Across from the second empty seat on their side.

Laura stood behind the other one.

She smiled up at him, and Connor was sure his weak knees were going to dump him on the floor right then and there.

"Guess we lost the game of musical chairs," she said, then went on in a lower voice. "Or did we win it?"

He laughed much louder than he intended to at that, and made a panic decision to get himself further away from everyone who heard it.

"One last switch?" he said, stepping back and pulling her chair out. "I'd bet you and my Mom could solve all of Wolf Branch's funding problems for the library before we're ready for dessert."

This time Laura laughed out loud, and Connor was mortified to giggle along with her. She sat, blushing all the way to her wonderful, delicate collarbones.

Linda was watching the two of them as he sat, a curious expression in her eyes.

Laura's mother finally set the long-held tray down in a forest of autumn leaf candles. Connor's stomach perked up at the little pieces of bread with pear slices and soft cheese on top.

"Well," she said, "now that the difficult matter of seating is at last resolved, it's my pleasure to welcome you all to Wolf Branch. I so seldom have the chance to host a more formal dinner party even though I teach men and women how to do so almost every day."

Connor's dad leaned forward, his pale blue eyes twinkling. Connor did everything he could to focus on his words and merry expression rather than how close his leg, his arm, his hand was to Laura.

"You teach at the high school?" his dad said. "Or at the college?"

"Or online?" Connor's mother said with one of her strange little smiles. The one that meant she knew the answer before she asked the question.

"I do teach online, yes," Laura's mother said, beaming. "At the high school and small groups in person sometimes, but mainly online. Interior decorating courses, usually for adults, but they get college credit."

Laura leaned toward Connor and spoke loud enough for only him to hear.

"From what I hear Dad say, her teaching covers her shopping habit. As far as I'm concerned, her shopping habit keeps her occupied."

He leaned forward to get each of them one of the appetizers, making sure to pretend interest in the conversation now well underway between their parents and Linda.

"Funny how that changes over time, isn't it? All those years keeping us busy and occupied. Now the tables have turned."

Laura looked him just enough to wink.

Connor recovered in time to catch his own name in the general conversation. Laura's father had joined them, leaving a plate of the best-looking grilled chicken he'd ever seen (or smelled), perfectly browned and juicy and dotted with spices. Her mother had disappeared along with the appetizer plate.

"I'm sorry," he said. "I was distracted by that amazing chicken."

Connor wasn't sure if the laughter around the table was a bit knowing, or if he was paranoid. Or maybe guilty. Linda brushed back a bit of loose hair.

"I was just asking about your work. In architecture, isn't it?"

Laura looked at him over her shoulder, with a smartass

grin and one raised eyebrow. That somehow got to him even more than her wink did.

"I studied architecture, yes," he said, struggling to keep a straight face. "Got my bachelors a few years ago. I've been working more on the building side, though, getting my hands into the work for a while."

Laura's father nodded slowly, with a tiny smile that made Connor like him immediately. He'd barely spent any time with Trish's parents, or she with his. He didn't think either of them felt as comfortable in that situation as he and Laura did right now.

"I'm glad to hear that, Connor," her father said. "About getting to know both sides of the business, sure. But to tell you the truth, I've got a long list of projects I could sure use some help with."

Before the laughter died down enough for Connor to answer, Laura's mother walked out with a huge bowl shaped like a bright yellow squash, complete with leaves and twirly bits of vines. Besides being pretty much adorable, it was stuffed full of salad greens in every color from palest green to orange to almost blood red.

"Don't let him get you roped in, Connor," she said, putting the bowl beside Linda. "Rick will have you working dawn to dusk, more if you don't watch him. He's supposed to be on a project *break*, anyway."

In the midst of Rick's protest and more laughter, Laura leaned close enough that her shoulder touched Connor's, setting off warm ripples through his body.

"Turns out Dad's project habit doesn't pay for itself the way Mom's does. But she doesn't mind all that much, since he can easily be detoured into working on *her* projects."

"Must be the trick to a long, happy marriage," he whispered back, close enough to smell the faint, sweet perfume of her hair. "My list at Mom and Dad's house has been growing by the day. It's almost like they don't expect me to go back to Chicago at all."

The meal went on that way, with the two of them participating in the main conversation from time to time, but far more focused on the sweet, silly, and secret dialog between them. Connor found himself floating in a haze of a hard day's work, great food, and the heady closeness growing with Laura.

Linda yanked him back to hard, cold reality with an innocent question as everyone was finishing up Patty's unbelievable apple and cranberry cobbler.

"How's Jim doing, Laura? He's nearly through over in Hidden Springs, thinking of going on to UVA for his doctorate after that?"

Everyone else at the table fell silent, and Linda looked puzzled for a second before her own face went pale.

Laura moved away from Connor. Only a tiny bit, and he had no right under the circumstances or by anyone's rules to wish she hadn't.

Certainly not with his own undefined relationship status.

But he still wished she hadn't.

Chapter 11

"Doing well," Laura said, cold bursting up from her belly and taking over the rest of her, nodding and staring at one of the guttering golden leaf candles in front of her. "He's doing well. He is planning to go on to UVA, that's right. Not sure if he'll be there for the fall semester or in January. Great place to study political science, so he's excited about that."

Laura knew she should look up at Linda, across the table to Connor's father or to her right to his mother. Maybe to her own father, who seemed quite taken with Connor and both his parents.

She wasn't sure whether it would be a worse idea to look at Connor himself or her own mother.

She settled for a cautious, cowardly half-look toward Linda.

"Well good," Linda said, nodding herself now. "That's good, and he's right. UVA is a great school for that. I hope… hope that goes really well for him."

"Would anyone like more coffee?" Laura's mother said, discomfort clear even through her well-practiced hostess voice. "Or I can mix up something else if you'd like. A hot toddy or hot buttered rum?"

No one spoke, and a hot, uncomfortable surge of guilt followed the cold in Laura's belly. She'd been sitting here flirting with Connor, shamelessly enough that everyone at the table had obviously noticed.

All while she let Jim put his education on hold because she couldn't make up her mind. Or maybe because she didn't want to.

And Connor had a girlfriend himself, Trish, wasn't it? He hadn't exactly declared he'd be leaving her behind in Chicago and running down to Wolf Branch in some grand romantic gesture.

But he *had* been flirting right back, hadn't he?

She dared glance at him, but he had his head turned away.

"I think a hot toddy sounds wonderful," Connor's father said, his smile a little sad.

"Some of Linda's apple cider for me," his mother said. "Can I help you, Patty? At least carry things back and forth?"

Laura watched her mother stand, and she could see her putting on her Gracious Hostess face. The one Laura could dismiss and sometimes even dislike when she was frustrated. In those moments, she could put that expression and the polite refusals of help all down to her mother wanting to be The Most Put Upon or The Martyr or something equally unflattering.

She suspected that was the truth, sometimes.

Then her mother froze in place, not breathing, and still enough that it seemed impossible a heart could be beating inside of her. She looked at Connor's parents, at Connor, and last of all at Laura.

She smiled and nodded.

"That would be a great help, Anne. Thank you."

Deep inside her embarrassment at so clearly being caught out and her utter confusion at how to feel about that, Laura was sad she couldn't even manage to share a wide-eyed look of shock with her father.

And she admitted to herself again that in those moments, her mother truly did want her guests to enjoy themselves, and she wanted to take care of them. Laura admired and wanted to emulate that trait as much as she could.

If she managed to survive whatever was going on tonight.

Connor's mother helped tally requests for three ciders and two hot toddies. Only Connor and Laura hadn't answered yet.

Because it could have gone no other way, they said "Coffee, please," at exactly the same time.

"Evan, you mentioned wanting to help folks get started with beekeeping," Laura's dad said, scooting his chair back. "Mind to take a look at our garden and flowers, see where you think might be best? I know Patty would adore having fresh honey all her own for those hot toddies, maybe even beeswax for these candles she loves so much."

Connor's father pushed his chair back and stood, watching Connor the whole time.

"Happy to, Rick. The honey and wax are a side benefit, really, compared with how much better everything will grow."

Linda was on her feet before they made it to the screen door.

"I'd love to see how you and Patty laid everything out this year," she said. "Her designs alone can get kids to pay more attention to what I'm trying to teach them."

And they were gone.

Laura took a deep, shaky breath. The easiest thing might be to jump up herself, and either go help her mother or join her father on the grand tour.

But some part of her knew that would actually be the hardest thing.

She turned and looked right into Connor's lovely green eyes.

"Strange how they all ran out at once like that," he said with a half-smile.

"Oh yeah, mysterious indeed. How will we *ever* discover the truth?"

He laughed under his breath despite her harsher-than-intended tone.

"Think we'll laugh about it someday? Like they always told us when we were kids?"

Laura rolled her eyes and relaxed the tiniest bit.

"I certainly hope so." She was drawing breath to ask if he wanted to join in on the garden tour when she heard the unmistakable *thrum-thrum-thrum* of his phone vibrating in his pocket.

The way he squeezed his eyes closed for a second told her who was calling.

"It's okay," she said. "Go ahead and answer. I'll go help…someone."

"No, no, voicemail can get it. I don't want to…"

Laura bit back her first response before it could escape her mind. What, admit you have a girlfriend? Even after we all got reminded about my boyfriend, *including* me?

She smiled, hoping it didn't look as fake as it felt.

"Really, go ahead. I'll let Mom know we've dispersed into the garden."

She got up before he could answer, and before the phone could start ringing again. His mother—Anne—met her at the sliding glass door with two orange and green coffee cups in hand.

"Thought I'd bring these out instead of making you two wait on…"

Her brow wrinkled for a second, and Laura was sure shadows crossed her eyes. They looked so much like Connor's that Laura's breath caught.

"Thank you, Anne," Laura said, taking one of the coffees. "I'll help Mom with the rest. The others, they're out in the garden now."

Laura turned toward her bedroom rather than the kitchen, meaning to dump the coffee and wash her face and try to calm down. The last thing she needed was caffeine when she was trying to get hold of the absurd ideas racing around and clamoring for attention inside her head.

Her mother's voice stopped her before she'd taken two steps.

"Laura? Are you okay?"

She turned and walked into the kitchen instead. She stared into her steaming hot cup of coffee, breathing in the fantastic scent to try to clear her mind

"I'm okay, Mom. Just needed to step inside for a second. Everyone else is out in the garden now."

She looked up to see her mother turning away from the five matching mugs lined up on the sparking tan granite counter, three of them already full of aromatic cider. Rather than disapproving at how Laura had abandoned their guests, she looked worried and a little sad.

"Connor too?"

Laura let out a breath and shook her head.

"No, not Connor. I expect he's talking to his girlfriend right now."

"Just felt the need to call her?"

Laura shook her head and tried to smile.

"No, I think *she* felt the need to call *him*."

She bit back another response that was surely best left unsaid.

Maybe Trish has radar and knew it was time to make herself visible, or at least audible.

Her mother nodded as she slowly poured hot water into the other two mugs. Laura felt the reflexive ache in her jaws after countless times of getting her Mom's amazing hot sour/sweet/strong/soothing toddies as much-needed medicine, adjusted for strength as she got older, naturally.

"Feeling any need to call Jim?" she said, floating an almost paper-thin lemon slice with a clove right in the middle on top of each toddy.

Laura checked inside to make sure before she answered, not wanting to get angry at what her mother *hadn't* said again. She'd overlaid the cloud of "Shouldn't you feel the need to call Jim?" quite nicely on her own.

"Not really, Mom. Not right this second."

Soft footsteps let them both know Anne had returned.

"I'll get these out to the garden," she said, and waited while Laura's mother took one of the hot toddies off the tray. "Thank you, Patty. These smell fantastic."

"You're quite welcome, Anne." She waited, breathing in the steam of her cocktail, until Anne left. "Did you hear from Jim today?"

Laura was surprised to have to stop and think about it. She'd gotten so busy with work and getting excited and worried about dinner that she hadn't realized she'd never gotten a call or text message or anything at all from him.

"I didn't hear from him, no."

"Don't you usually?"

Laura took a sip of coffee, the hot, earthy taste calming her nerves more than she expected.

"Yeah, Mom. I usually hear from him sometime during the day."

Their eyes met, and for a long moment, Laura was thirteen years old, right after the awful experience of her first crush. Begging her mother to explain why it hurt so much that he didn't love her back.

No matter how she'd been flirting with Connor—or how she'd been feeling about him—Jim was supposed to love her back. Or at least love her.

Fair or not, this hurt too.

"That's a pretty big turnaround for him from last night," her mother said. "Jim, I mean."

"Wait, he said he couldn't make it tonight. Didn't he? And aren't you on Team Jim anyway?"

Her mother let out a soft snort and rolled her eyes.

"I didn't know there were teams," she said. "And I never heard whether he could make it tonight or not. I did get loud and clear that *you* didn't want him to be here."

She walked toward the door, then looked at Laura over her shoulder.

"I like Jim, you know that. I always have. You two seemed good together. But if we're going to have teams, Laura, I'm always going to be on yours."

She'd been gone long enough for the coffee to get cold before Laura realized her mother had said they *seemed* good together, in the past tense.

Maybe her mother had realized more than Laura knew, last night and tonight.

Maybe it was past time Laura did the same.

Chapter 12

Connor sat on the neat, perfectly level concrete steps going down into the Michaelson's back yard, not sure when, where, or even *if* he should call Trish back.

The sweet scent of what he would have sworn was jasmine rose around him, but all he could see close by were mounds of mums in every color under the sun. Just like all the flowerbeds and shrubs and trees he saw throughout the huge yard, the mums were coordinated and arranged with an artist's eye rather than the sterile demonstration units he'd thought of earlier.

Whether he could see it or not, jasmine so late into the season in a cold climate didn't make much sense. Just like all kinds of things weren't making sense to him right now.

His mom had passed by a few minutes ago, with nothing more than a squeeze of his shoulder on the way out to the garden.

Waiting for Laura to walk by, or talk to him, or join him on the steps felt equal measures stupid and pathetic. Certainly when he knew his…girlfriend or good friend or friend with benefits was trying to reach him. Even more so when Laura was probably inside talking to Boyfriend Jim.

He scrubbed his hands through his hair, not nearly as worried about how it looked as he'd been half an hour ago. That lasted until he heard soft footsteps behind him. He could only hope he managed to smooth it down enough to be presentable.

"I hope you enjoyed the coffee," Laura's mother said, passing by him and going down the five steps.

Connor glanced at the cup he'd carefully placed on the step beside him. He'd almost forgotten drinking it, but he did remember how good it was.

"I did, Mrs. Michaelson. It was delicious, like everything else. Everything was wonderful. Thank you for inviting us."

She smiled and tilted her head to the side.

"My pleasure, Connor. Please do call me Patty."

"I'll do my best."

She finished a hot toddy that smelled amazing, all lemon and clove and whiskey, and left the cup beside Connor's.

"Planning to join us for the impromptu garden tour? Let Rick get a head start on his project list for you?"

Connor laughed and shook his head even though nothing about the current situation felt at all amusing. He felt like he had to make sure she didn't know that.

"Maybe we can talk it over another time," he said. "Mom and Dad will keep him plenty busy. Listen, can I ask you a question? Patty?"

He waited for her to nod.

"Did you bring out pots of jasmine from a greenhouse or something? I'd swear I'm smelling it, but I thought it would be too cold already."

She smiled, looking about twenty years old. Looking more like Laura than he'd realized before.

"Would you believe that's sweet potato vine?" she said, pointing to a wooden lattice under the porch that he hadn't noticed. "The potato part isn't good for anything but growing the vine, but these late season blooms that smell so wonderful are a cool-weather gardener's best friend. Speak to you later."

The lattice on both sides of the steps was covered with a spray of small white flowers that looked as much like jasmine as they smelled. But the leaves were shaped more like an oak than the rounded leaves of jasmine he'd seen before. Just one more way Patty made her home comforting and pleasant.

He hadn't quite decided between wandering off to find his parents or going inside to try to find Laura when his phone rang again. At least the simple act of answering it didn't require much thought.

"*There* you are!" Trish said in full exuberant mode. "What are you into on this beautiful mountain evening?"

"Hey Trish. Just finishing up dinner with my parents and some of the local folks. Mom and Dad will probably work with them on a few projects. I might too."

He had to strain to hear her over an unusually loud connection. Or maybe she was in wind, or even driving.

"Sounds lovely. Any good food I should know about?"

"Well, sure," he said, getting to his feet and wandering away from the porch. "I mean, home cooking, you know. But good."

His guilt at downplaying both Rick and Patty's fantastic cooking skills surprised him as much as the urge to do it had. Too late to take it back now.

"Fantastic. Maybe I'll get to meet them."

Everything inside Connor turned to ice.

"Get to… Trish, where are you?"

She laughed in exactly the same light and free way he'd always so enjoyed hearing.

Right now, she may as well have been shrieking a bad song off-key.

"If my phone is telling me the truth, I'm about twenty minutes away from you."

His mind relentlessly played her words back.

This beautiful mountain evening. And the noisy connection.

He closed his eyes and rubbed his forehead.

"That's great, Trish, what a surprise. What made you… Never mind that, we can talk when you get here. The house is pretty small, Mom and Dad's, but I'm sure we'll manage."

"Connor, I might be bold enough to drive down and surprise you, but even I wouldn't invite myself to stay in your parents' brand-new place. I have a room at a hotel in town. The Wolf Song. Have you seen it?"

Connor switched to squeezing his temples.

"Yeah, I've seen it. That's where we were when you called last night. Seems like a nice place. I…wow, I'm not sure what to say."

She was silent for several seconds, and he finally straightened up and opened his eyes. He'd managed to get about ten feet away from the steps.

When he turned to walk back, Laura was sitting there waiting for him.

"Well, I expected you to say you were excited about seeing me," Trish said, disappointment clear in her voice despite the rough connection. "You certainly don't *sound* like you are."

Connor fought the urge to run, or at least to dart around the side of the house and into the street. Excited was nowhere near the list of words he'd use

"I'm sorry, Trish, we had a long day working at the house today. You know I'm excited, of course I am. I'll have to go to the house to get my things. Maybe let me know what your room number is and I'll meet you there as soon as I can?"

"That's a date." Her voice was still cool, but not as bad as before. "Don't worry, I won't keep you up all night. We've got three nights to make up for it."

He slipped his phone back into his pocket, took a deep breath, and walked slowly toward the porch.

With luck, Laura would have spoken to the Boyfriend Jim, even though Connor didn't love that idea. He very much wanted to be friends with her if…

If nothing else.

"Everything still calm out here?" she said, smiling up at him.

"More or less. How about inside?"

She shrugged, rubbing at one of her shoulders. He tried not to stare at her collarbones or anything else.

"I don't know. Things are strange, I can say that." She took a deep breath. "I hope I didn't interrupt your phone call."

"All finished," he said. And then he had no idea what to say next. When the silence stretched on long enough, she tried again.

"Want to go for a walk, then? See the much-discussed garden for yourself?"

Connor wanted to shrink into the ground and disappear, or maybe crawl up inside one of those potato blooms. He wasn't sure who he was more worried about hurting. Trish or Laura.

Either way, he figured his own feelings would be collateral damage.

"I have to get going, actually. As soon as I can find Mom and Dad. That call, that was Trish letting me know she drove down to visit me. To surprise me. She's in town now."

Laura raised her eyebrows, and Connor was certain he saw all the breath leaving her.

"That *is* a surprise. I'll let you get to that." She stood and started up the steps.

"Laura? I hope… I don't have any idea how to say this. I really like spending time with you. Maybe we can… I mean, it would be great if all four of us could be friends."

Laura nodded slowly, and now her smile was tight and uncomfortable.

"Sure, Connor." She picked up the two mugs and glanced back at him. "That sounds great."

She walked inside, leaving him wondering why his heart felt colder than the evening air.

Chapter 13

By the time Laura made it less than a minute's walk to her bedroom, her fingers and hands and wrists and arms ached from clenching her fists. She closed the door behind her, clutched the fuzzy blue housecoat hanging on the back of it against her face, and yelled out a good, hearty *FUCK* as loud as she could.

She breathed deep for a few seconds, listening to her heart pounding in her ears. She'd never had an evening, a day, or anything else go from so good to so bad so fast.

She dropped the housecoat and turned around, pounding her head against the door a few times for good measure.

The room didn't look like such a dipshit lived in it. Walls painted a soothing indigo once she'd outgrown little girl pink, but was still young enough to want to annoy her mother. Laura liked it enough now that she had no plans to change it. Curtains that matched, same with the rugs covering the hardwood floor.

Everything on the bed was closer to sky blue, and shelves all over the wall covered with books of every size and color brightened it up even more.

Didn't look like the room of a girl young enough to feel this twisted up and messed up by a guy, either.

She walked over and flopped onto the bed, covering her eyes with her arm.

"Real smooth, Laura. You *knew* he was talking to his girlfriend out there. And you still had to go charging in to see if he might like you best anyway?"

She couldn't pretend, even inside her room and inside her own head, that she didn't hope or even wish Connor did like her best.

After knowing him for almost no time at all, that didn't make sense. And it was still true.

She shook her head and turned onto her side. No matter how much she might want her mind to shut down and let her sleep or read or at least think about something else, she knew this would take a while to work through. Her thoughts had a determined, almost manic quality she recognized all too well.

And what the hell was up with Jim? Between him and her mother, Laura had been scared to death he was going to propose or some other such nonsense just last night. And now he was what? Giving her some space?

She'd never known him to do that the whole time they'd been dating. That had been part of the trouble.

She sat up, then kicked off her shoes and grabbed her phone.

At least this one thing she could reasonably expect an answer to. And she could reasonably get one tonight.

He waited until the third ring to pick up, because otherwise the whole thing might have been easier.

"Hi Laura. How was the big dinner?"

"Jim. It was fine. Nice people. Had a busy day?"

He paused for a second, and she was sure she heard him counting to ten under his breath.

"Not all that busy, no. Working on a paper and presentation, helping out around the house."

Now Laura wanted to stop and count to ten herself.

"*That's* why you couldn't make it to dinner tonight?"

"No. Well, yeah. I guess that is why. I just…needed a break, I think."

Laura jumped up and started pacing around her bedroom, sock feet padding on carpet, the wood, then carpet again.

She wondered if Connor was still outside.

"A break from me?" she said.

"That's part of it, sure. Listen, I don't want to get into this over the phone. Want to talk tomorrow?"

"Not really, Jim. I'd rather not have this on my mind all night long. It's only eight. Are you so busy you can't meet me for a little while?"

This time she heard him muttering to himself for sure.

"I've got class tomorrow."

Before she could stop herself, Laura laughed out loud. Hard as Jim worked at school, he'd always managed to have time to cut loose in the evenings. She'd been the same way, and that was *why* she worked so hard.

"You have class at eleven tomorrow, one you could sleep through and still get an A. And it's virtual classroom. You'll do it from your bedroom in shorts and a t-shirt. Is meeting me really that much to ask?"

For a second, Laura was certain Jim would say it was. That it was indeed far too much to ask, even after they'd been friends for ages and dated for two years.

The scary thing was she half hoped he *would* say that.

"It's a lot to ask," he said, but she heard the smile in his voice. "But I guess it's not *too* much. Where? Town square?"

Laura pictured the glorified grassy field that somehow got preserved and left empty for nothing more than the occasional award ceremony and holiday events. She'd heard serious discussions about building something there, a new church probably, maybe a couple of houses.

A few people might be there, but it was getting too chilly for any kind of big crowds.

"Works for me. See you there in ten minutes."

She refused to dress up or dress down or even check her hair, not after all the fuss and bother she'd gone through before dinner. She grabbed a light jacket and started toward her door, then paused with her hand on the cool brass doorknob.

What if Connor and his family were walking out at exactly the same time? She wouldn't mind seeing Anne and Evan again one little bit, and she hoped seeing Connor again would be acceptable before too much time passed.

But right that second, the idea of seeing him felt like sandpaper on bone.

Laura did her best to ignore how relieved she was to get through the house and out the door without seeing anyone at all.

Chapter 14

The door to room 207 at the Wolf Song hotel wasn't especially remarkable. A little wider than most hotel doors, a good thirty-eight inches to Connor's practiced eye. Solid, light-colored pine, nice knots and variations.

The hardware and sideways curve of the handle were a darkened oil-rubbed bronze, the gleaming metal a perfect contrast for all the wood in the door and the floor under his feet. The number was the same metal set into the door at his eye level. Two zero seven.

Trish's room. Impossible to miss or mistake.

And still Connor stood, frozen, nothing moving but his racing mind. No sound but his speeding heartbeat.

Patty Michaelson's wonderful coffee that he could still taste didn't account for all of his fast pulse and shaky hands. He shifted his brown overnight bag from one hand to the other yet again and looked up and down the hallway. No one else was out, but he heard a TV turn on behind one of those impressive doors.

His brain tried to play back the last couple of hours for at least the tenth time in the last five minutes, even though he knew he wouldn't find anything different. He and Laura had had a nice evening, that's all. Nothing wrong or even mildly scandalous about it.

They why did he keep fighting back wishes that she would be waiting for him here rather than Trish?

The next thought—of Trish calling to see where he was right now, right this second, where she would hear him talking—finally got him moving. He knocked, noticing how the door was so well-fitted that it didn't rattle in its frame at all. Didn't even matter that he knocked harder than he meant to.

He heard the distinctive sound of feet thumping on the floor just before the door swung back enough to reveal two light brown eyes. Enough so Connor saw the eyes and cheeks and lips curve in a smile even before it opened all the way.

"You're *finally* here!" Trish cried, laughing as she pulled him into a tight hug. "I was afraid you'd decided to go back to Chicago instead."

"Course I didn't. I don't have my truck, for one thing. And you're right here."

Trish grinned and pulled him into the room so she could close that heavy door. She wasn't wearing Connor's imagined lacy nightgown or even nothing at all. She wore jeans and a t-shirt with a long-sleeved shirt over it, and her short brown hair was caught back away from her face with a fuzzy blue headband.

And yes, she looked adorable.

The room itself was bigger than he'd expected, made of the same sturdy, often reclaimed materials as the rest of the building. A wardrobe made of marked and pitted pine, shelves supported by dark metal pipes, all of it creating a rustic and stylish effect.

Connor was more relieved than he wanted to admit that

a small tile-topped round table and two chairs sat along one wall.

That way they had somewhere besides the four-poster king-sized bed to talk.

"What took you so long?" Trish leaned up to kiss his cheek, then flopped into one of the chairs.

"I had to get Mom and Dad back home, get my things, then get a ride back into town with a friend of theirs. One of the teachers out at the high school."

"Well, we have my rental car now. Is their house nice?" She shivered. "How far out in the middle of nowhere do they live?"

Trish had never lived outside of Chicago, not even as far out as the suburbs. She wasn't exactly a fan of camping or getting out into the wilderness.

"They're a good fifteen minutes outside Wolf Branch. The house really is out in the middle of the woods. It's quiet and cozy and lovely. Trish, what made you decide to drive all the way down here?"

She shrugged and smiled at the same time.

"I don't know. One professor was out until next week, a seminar got canceled, and everything else was calm for a change. It just seemed like a good chance to get away for an adventure."

She held out her hand palm up on the blue and yellow tiles. Connor took it almost reflexively, and the warmth of her skin was pleasant against the cool surface.

"And I missed you, okay?" she said, and her cheeks turned pink. "Even when I'm insanely busy, I guess I've kind of gotten used to having you around."

He managed to smile, but the clashing thoughts in his mind and feelings in his heart weren't making it easy. He and Trish got along just fine, aside from the sex, which was fantastic. He hadn't thought much about anything else since they both stayed busy talking about how they were just friends.

But would it be so bad to have more of a proper relationship with her? A smart, beautiful, ambitious young woman who happened to be great in bed? And who apparently liked him enough to drive ten hours to surprise him?

Hell, he could go back to Chicago with her, too, no need to worry about his own rental.

The thing was he knew he would have felt differently just a couple of days ago. Before he met Laura.

Laura, who was probably out with Boyfriend Jim right this second.

"I'm glad to see you, Trish. This was a great surprise."

She leaned across the table enough to kiss him, but only a quick little peck.

"Then let's get out of here. Take me for a walk and show me the town. I hope you have time to take a drive with me tomorrow. I've never seen anything like the mountains I saw in Kentucky before it got dark."

Connor drew back, opening his mouth and closing it before he managed to speak.

"Sure, we can go for a walk if you want. Nothing much is open this late besides the restaurant downstairs and the brewery across town. Not that it takes more than a few minutes to walk across town. You want to go now?"

She stood and pulled him up after her, then stepped into his arms.

"I'd *love* to go now. I've been sitting in a car all day, remember? Once we see at least a few of the sights, we can come back here and go to bed. I really have missed you, Connor."

He hugged her tight and whispered into her ear, "It's so great to see you."

Trish looked at him with the slightest wrinkle in her

brow when she drew back, but she started talking about her drive before they left the room.

The distraction of a stroll around Wolf Branch—with at least the faint possibility of gathering his scattered wits about him—was about the best idea Connor had ever heard.

Chapter 15

Laura pulled on an old Wolf Branch high school sweat-shirt when she got out of her car, wondering why she hadn't noticed before how aged and frayed the shirt was. The gray had faded to almost white, and the formerly tight-knit cuffs around her wrists were loose and misshapen.

Not exactly the most flattering thing she owned, not by a long shot. But it was the only warm thing hanging by the front door that she could grab on her way out.

She didn't care nearly as much about flattering as she had a few hours ago, getting ready for dinner. She'd taken extra care before seeing Connor.

Not so much to see Jim. Laura wasn't sure what that meant yet, if anything.

She shook her head and locked the car as she walked away.

The field was only a few hundred feet across, about half a town block, with sidewalk on three sides. Streetlights that looked like double gas lamps were set at intervals, but a bit of fog in the air kept them from doing a whole lot of good.

A couple of other cars were parked along the street, but no one else was out here. No one at all.

Not even Jim.

Laura was more angry than she wanted to admit about that. He only lived a couple of blocks away, in a reassuringly typical bachelor apartment over the garage at his parents' house. He could have walked here and back more than once in the time it took for her to get ready and drive down here.

She walked across the grass anyway, toward the Wolf Song hotel and restaurant. Pretty much the only things open at this time of night. Better to stay down here for a while alone than go running back home. Dew kicked up onto her jeans immediately and started to soak through, and the scent of roasting meat from the restaurant lingered in the still air.

A few wooden benches lined the edges of the space. Nothing spectacular or even especially comfortable. They'd mostly been rescued from the town park down by the river, when they'd gotten new ones installed a few years back.

She'd spent time down here with her friends growing up, and more than one boyfriend as she got older. Running around like fools playing catch or kicking around a soccer ball. Sitting shoulder to shoulder on the grass and gossiping and giggling.

Snuggled up on the same grass or the benches with one boy or another. Talking and laughing, holding hands and learning how to kiss. Helping with 4-H or Girl Scouts projects, building the rectangular planters between the benches that held masses of colorful mums this time of year.

Laura sat carefully on the bench opposite the hotel, making sure not to get a splinter in her hands or backside. What a perfect way to end an evening that had started out with so much excitement and promise. Now it was nothing but confusion and upset.

She turned at a voice from behind her.

"Sure it's safe to be out here alone, miss?"

Jim walked along the sidewalk, hands in his pockets, dressed in his usual nighttime sweatpants and a t-shirt with a hoodie.

"It was safe when I was alone," she said, smiling to soften her words. "Did you get lost between here and your house?"

He shook his head as he sat beside her, crossing his ankles and staring down at them.

"Naaah, I know the way. I also know the way it's good to give you time to think when you're upset."

Laura looked over at him, but he still focused on his own feet.

"Time to think, huh? Because I'm so irrational or something like that?"

He shook his head again. "Because you told me once that you hated being forced to talk when you weren't ready to. So I try not to."

She blinked and looked away, surprised he'd paid that much attention. Her gaze caught motion outside the hotel. Another couple walking across the street.

"Thank you, Jim. I do appreciate it. I'm ready to talk now."

He finally glanced at her for a second.

"Yeah, you seem pretty calm. Okay, what do you want to talk about?"

"I don't know. Why I never heard from you today? Why you said you couldn't make it to dinner when you were home all day? Why you were so dressed up last night?"

He grunted out laughter, and Laura couldn't help laughing herself.

"Is that all?" he said.

"Like I said, I don't know. I just feel like we both probably have a lot to say, but we're not saying much of anything."

He shrugged without taking his hands out of his pockets.

"It's been like that for a while, hasn't it? Both of us not saying what we want to?"

Now hot tears welled up in Laura's throat and eyes. Feeling bored and upset and frustrated with Jim was one thing.

Having him admit he hadn't been happy either raised the stakes considerably.

"I thought we were both busy," she said. "Something like that. I figured we'd get caught up sometime soon."

Jim took a deep breath, then he glanced up at the couple walking through the fog a block away, between the streetlights.

"Me too. Or else we'd just...decide to make a change. That's why I was dressed up last night, Laura. I wanted to ask you to come to Charlottesville with me."

"Jim, I'm not sure about school, you know that. I might want—"

"I do know that. You might not have noticed, but I didn't say *anything* about you going to school. Not last night and not just now."

Laura closed her eyes, once again upset with herself for reacting to what another person *hadn't* said.

"No, you didn't say that. I'm sorry. Want to tell me why you didn't ask me last night?"

He shifted, sitting up beside her, but still not looking at her.

"I don't like admitting this, for the record. Not any more than I liked feeling it. You made it pretty clear you didn't want me around, remember? Pretty clear that you *did* want this new guy around. What was his name? Colin?"

Laura tried to ignore the slow, lazy loop her stomach turned at the thought of her wanting the new guy. She was afraid that feeling wasn't going to disappear anytime soon.

"Connor. His name is Connor. I just wanted to welcome them to town, that's all. But I am sorry about how I acted, Jim. I wasn't having the best mental health day yesterday."

"Big mess inside your head?" he said, leaning over enough to nudge her shoulder with his.

"Disaster area is more like it. I'd say it needs a total shutdown. A week at least."

"So you're not saying no to coming with me. But you *are* saying you still need to think about it."

Laura turned to look at him, and she was relieved when he turned to meet her gaze.

"I am. Is that okay?"

Jim kissed the corner of her mouth and nodded once.

"It is. I think we'll do a whole hell of a lot better once we get out of here and really start our lives."

Laura closed her eyes, not wanting to try to explain to him again how much her work in Wolf Branch was starting to mean to her. When he moved to put his arm around her, she scooted closer and rested her head against his shoulder.

The soft murmur of conversation approaching from their left registered on her ears only a couple of seconds before one voice resolved in her mind. The same voice that had been whispering into her ear all through dinner.

That was Connor.

Talking to a woman.

Laura resisted as long as she could, until she was certain Connor would recognize her first. And until her heart and stomach knotted up at the idea of him seeing her sitting so close to Jim.

She shifted her head and opened her eyes.

As it turned out, seeing Connor with his arm around a beautiful woman knotted her stomach up a hell of a lot worse.

Chapter 16

Walking through the cool, foggy night with Trish cleared Connor's mind more than he would have thought possible. If nothing else, the clear, quiet air helped push away the agitation that had lodged in his mind like a splinter under his skin.

Wolf Branch was lovely at night, too. The double street-lights gave just enough light to make a magical glow, and the neat sidewalks and brick buildings looked like movie set miniatures, or maybe someone's overgrown model railroad set.

Even with no one else out, he'd been at small town slow pace long enough to want to go right to the open grassy area not far from the restaurant. The lack of lights in the middle might have made it seem ominous on another night, in another mood. But right now the wispy bits of fog twisting through turned it into an inviting fairyland.

He started that way, but Trish linked her arm through his.

"Show me all the sweet little shops I'll be exploring while

I'm here. I almost never have time to even window shop these days."

He couldn't argue with how busy she'd been. Trish's constant workload with law school had done its part to help turn Connor away from getting into grad school himself.

They headed up the sidewalk instead, following the gentle grade up toward the high school and the cannery, lights from both popping in and out of view as the fog shifted.

The strange contrast of walking on the same cozy sidewalk with Trish hit him. Walking past the same rows of neatly maintained brick buildings that he'd walked past and gone into more times than he could count. With his parents and grandparents and aunts and uncles and cousins.

Doing such an ordinary thing with an almost-girlfriend who'd never been here before filled him with an odd sense of satisfying dislocation.

"Tell me about Wolf Branch, Connor. I've heard you talk about it, but seeing it changes everything."

Connor smiled and shook his head. That was something else she hardly ever seemed to have time for lately. Talking with him rather than *at* him, especially when it came to him going back to school. Asking about him, listening to him.

Making him feel like something besides The Patient and Sympathetic (Sort of) Boyfriend.

"I'm hardly the expert, you'll want my Dad or some of the people I've met for that. But I'll do my best."

He stopped and turned to look back the way they'd come, putting his arm around Trish as she turned with him.

"It's hard to see tonight with the fog, but Wolf Branch pretty much sits in a bowl of mountains. See the orange lights up on the hill beyond the hotel? That's the hospital. Mom and Dad were born in Illinois, but all our family in town were born right there."

He waved his arm down toward the left. "Down there is the source of all the water in the air right now, the Grasspe River. We'll have to be sure and go down there before you leave. Hiking, canoeing, rafting. It's beautiful with the leaves this time of year. There are all kinds of rare plants too, but Dad definitely knows more about that than me."

They turned back and kept walking, and Connor spotted another couple across the grass, sitting close together on a bench. A strong desire to avoid them surprised him.

"What do people here *do* besides all the outdoor stuff?" Trish said. "To make a living, I mean."

He managed to fight back an exasperated sigh as they turned the corner, walking uphill again along the shorter side of the field.

And he pushed away the memory of Laura talking about her work with the town, how she was so clearly excited to be making a difference. How her eyes and face lit up, somehow even more beautiful.

"People here do a lot of the same things they do everywhere," he said. "There's tourism, sure. But there are doctors and lawyers and teachers, people running businesses. There's a college less than an hour away, a bigger one and an art school not much further off. One of the people I had dinner with tonight teaches interior design online. It's not like we're entirely cut off from the outside world."

"We, huh?" Trish said, raising her eyebrows. "Made some decisions I need to know about?"

"Not that I know of. There *is* life outside of Chicago, that's all. Mom's going to be helping out with the library, Dad's going to be teaching at the high school. They're both really interested in getting involved in the cannery."

He waved toward the high school, but a thicker drift of fog blocked those lights from view.

Trish didn't hide her annoyed sigh as well as he had. Or as well as he hoped he had, anyway. She stepped away from his arm.

"I guess I'll have to ask your Dad what on earth a cannery is, too. I'm not about to ask you with the way you just snapped at me."

Connor squeezed his eyes closed for a second, playing his words back in his mind. Yeah, he probably had gone a little overboard with his tone, if not his words. His parents had done everything they could to teach him how to avoid that when he was a snotty teenager, but it still slipped through sometimes.

"I'm sorry, Trish. That wasn't fair of me. A cannery is just what it sounds like, really. A place where people go to put up their preserves or pickles or whatever they have instead of steaming up their own kitchens. They used to be all over the place. In Illinois, too."

She watched him for a few seconds, hands on her hips. He recognized her expression: mouth tight on one side, eyes slightly narrowed. They didn't spend enough time together in their current arrangement for this evaluation of him to happen often. But he had no doubt she was trying to decide whether an argument was worth it.

She took a deep breath and let it out with a smile.

"I don't think I've ever eaten anything someone canned at home instead of buying it from the store. Maybe we can check it out and try something while I'm here?"

Connor held out his arm and she slipped her arm around his waist.

"You bet. We'll do that tomorrow. You'll have to taste real Appalachian apple butter, and on a fresh buttermilk biscuit. Probably couldn't find that in the city even if you tried."

They turned again, back down the hill toward the hotel.

Connor realized neither he nor Trish had been paying any attention to the neatly decorated shop windows they'd passed along the way, each creating its own little world in their lighted display.

He started to say so, then thought better of it. Maybe that had been an excuse to get out and still spend time with him. Or something else he couldn't figure out yet.

She confirmed his hunch a second later when she leaned up and kissed his cheek.

"We're not getting much window shopping done, are we? But my ploy to get you out with me on a romantic foggy night is working to perfection."

Every once in a while, he was pleasantly surprised that his guy mind caught a clue with a woman.

"I was wondering about that. Long drive for a stroll around a small town."

Trish leaned her head against his shoulder for a second.

"While I was on that long drive, I realized we haven't spent much time just…hanging out. Talking. Being friends. Not for ages. We've barely had time for the good stuff."

They'd almost drawn even with the couple still sitting on the bench, the guy closer than the woman, both of them facing toward the middle of the field.

An uneasiness Connor didn't understand tickled at his mind.

"We used to be friends, didn't we?" he said. "I mean, we still are, obviously, but you're right. It's good to have time to talk to you, Trish."

"Don't get me wrong. I plan to get plenty of the good stuff while I'm here." They laughed together. "But yeah, I'm really looking forward to spending time with you."

His gaze was drawn to movement from the couple ahead of them, as the woman shifted her head on the man's chest to look up at Connor.

The woman was Laura.

He almost tripped over his own two feet, possibly because that's where his heart ended up.

Chapter 17

Laura didn't realize how much she'd tensed up until Jim shifted away from her.

"You okay?"

She nodded and sat back, unable to take her eyes off Connor. And the gorgeous woman with her arm around him. Tall and slender and stunning in jeans and a long-sleeved shirt, and with thick brown hair pulled back from high cheekbones that could have easily been on a classical painting or statue of some kind.

"I'm okay," Laura said in a low voice before she spoke louder. "Hi Connor. Didn't expect to see you down here tonight."

The two of them stopped walking, but they didn't step away from each other.

"Hi Laura. Trish wanted to see a bit of the town. Trish Paretski, this is Laura Michaelson."

Laura only realized Jim's arm was still around her shoulders when it got tight enough to be uncomfortable. She got to her feet and held out her hand, putting on her best "Welcome to Wolf Branch" smile that she hoped wasn't showing too many teeth.

"I've heard quite a bit about you, Trish. I'm glad to meet you." Laura shook Trish's hand, impossibly slender and delicate and lovely, and warm, of course. "Trish, Connor, this is Jim Blevins."

Seeing Connor and Jim shake hands a little too vigorously—obviously sizing each other up—made Laura's heart and stomach feel like they were caught in a vise. She couldn't pretend beautiful Trish wasn't looking her up and down, either.

After a grip and stare that lasted an eternity, Jim let go and shook Trish's hand for a quick second.

"I've heard about you too, Connor," he said, his voice cold. "Nice to meet you, Trish. I hope you're enjoying your visit so far."

Trish stepped back, crossing her arms under her perfectly shaped breasts, perfect at least to Laura's uncomfortably jealous eye.

"I've only been here for a couple hours," she said. "Everyone's been really friendly. So far."

There it was, the flaw Laura was too ashamed to admit her mind was seeking. Trish had a clipped, sort of nasal voice, or maybe it was an accent. Either way, Connor didn't talk like that at all.

But he was obviously quite fond of someone who did.

"I hope you'll have time on your visit to see more of the area," Laura said, terribly self-conscious about her own slow, soft, Appalachian accent. "It's lovely this time of year."

Trish raised her eyebrows and flashed a tight smile.

"I'm sure I will. I get the feeling there's a lot to see."

"Don't let us keep you," Jim said, stepping back himself. "I was just leaving."

Connor finally looked into Laura's eyes, and she realized

he'd been avoiding that. Or maybe she had. This time the flash of heat between them felt like shame.

"We're about ready to head back," he said. "Nice to meet you, Jim. Good night."

He and Trish walked away together, but no longer with their arms around each other. Laura took a deep breath and turned back to Jim, still standing, but now with his hands on his hips.

"Nice couple," he said, staring after them. "You forgot to mention your new buddy Connor has a girlfriend. Or that she was here."

Laura shrugged, determined not to admit she hadn't wanted to think about Trish at all.

"It didn't occur to me. I wanted to see you, not talk about other people."

Jim ran his hands through his hair then looked at Laura.

"Is this why you don't want to go to Charlottesville with me? This guy you just met?"

"You *know* I already wasn't sure about school," Laura said, then she saw her opportunity. "That has nothing to do with Connor or you or anyone else besides me. I didn't say I *don't* want to go with you, though. I'm just...I'm not sure about anything right now."

He watched her for an endless moment, his face unreadable.

"So you're not saying yes..."

Laura shook her head. "And I'm not saying no. I need some time. Nothing has changed about that. Okay?"

Jim tipped his head back and took a deep breath, his typical way of calming himself down. Laura hoped he wouldn't ask any more questions. Certainly not about Connor.

Or about how she honestly wasn't sure how she felt about

moving to Charlottesville, but she *was* sure she didn't like seeing Connor and Trish walk away, now arm in arm again.

"Does this mean we're back to a couple of weeks to think about it?" Jim said.

Laura nodded, forcing herself not to watch the others disappear into the fog, into the hotel, and into a room together.

"That's where I am, Jim. I hope you can meet me there."

He smiled, and this time it was almost normal.

"Sure I can. Come on, I'll walk you back to your car. We could both stand to get some rest."

Laura fell into step beside him, straight out across the damp grass. After a few feet, she was glad to feel his arm go around her shoulders. On an impulse she couldn't explain and didn't want to argue with, she stopped and hugged him tight.

"Want company tonight?" she whispered. "Don't worry, I've got work tomorrow myself."

She felt his chest and stomach expand and he sighed warm and soft against her neck. The heat felt wonderful with the damp chill of the evening, and it even pushed away some of the snarl of confusion inside.

"Yeah, that would be great. I won't even have to shove the mess out of the way for a change. Had enough time on my hands to clean top to bottom today."

Laura grinned and stood on her tiptoes to kiss him soundly.

"Now I insist on coming over. I have to see that for myself."

They walked the rest of the way to her car laughing, as silly and close as they'd ever been. At least on the surface.

The bed in Jim's apartment was comfortable enough, and she'd stayed there plenty of times over the last couple of years. They were both usually plenty worn out and satisfied by the time they finally went to sleep.

But Laura strongly doubted she'd be sleeping much at all.

And if she did, she was afraid her dreams weren't going to be anywhere near sweet.

Chapter 18

Connor sat at the little yellow-and-blue-tiled coffee table
back in Trish's hotel room, running his fingertips along the
light gray grout lines between the squares. Nice and smooth,
that grout. Someone had taken care to put enough down to
begin with, then taken the time to level it out.

Focusing on that felt safe to him. Reassuring. Something
he was pretty good at, but he knew he could get better with
practice. Maybe as good as whoever had made this table.

He wasn't at all sure he was good at relationships, friends
with benefits or not. And he didn't feel the least bit confident
he'd ever get better at it.

Trish hadn't said a word on the walk back to the hotel,
though she'd slipped her arm around his waist again about
halfway there. As soon as they got to her room, she'd gone
into the bathroom and closed the door.

At least she hadn't slammed it.

He tilted his head to the left, then to the right, trying to
loosen up the muscles in his neck and shoulders. That
tension wasn't all because he'd worked so hard that day on
the shelves for his parents.

Could that have really been the same day, sitting at a round wooden table with his mother eating her cinnamon and ginger cookies? Between the dinner with Laura and her family that turned so strange, Trish showing up, and running into Laura again, Connor felt like at least a month had passed since he woke that morning.

He had no idea how long Trish had been in the bathroom. Minutes, hours. Maybe a whole day he'd managed to miss, sitting and staring at the careful grout lines.

He also had no idea if Trish had picked up on the discomfort of their little meeting with Laura and...Boyfriend Jim. Who'd turned out to be a big brute of a guy, easily six inches taller than Connor and built like a linebacker. Broad shoulders, strong arms and legs, and not afraid to deploy a crushing handshake.

One Connor had no trouble returning after years of working so hard with his own hands.

But all of that fell to the side with the quick, easy intelligence he'd recognized in Boyfriend Jim's eyes. No matter how he looked, he wasn't some nightmare dumb jock from a bad teenager movie.

No, this guy was smart *and* strong *and* good-looking, and from what Laura said, well on his way to a successful and impressive career.

Laura would be crazy to walk away from a guy like that.

Not that she'd said a word about wanting to.

The bathroom door opened, and Connor's body strongly suggested that he'd be plenty crazy to walk away from Trish, too.

She still wasn't wearing any sort of sexy lingerie or seductive nightgown, though he'd seen her in a bit of lacy nothing more than once. She wore a midnight blue t-shirt and matching shorts. Both loose and comfortable and doing not a damn thing to hide her lovely body and gorgeous long legs.

She leaned against the door frame and watched him, her head tilted to one side. She'd showered and let her damp hair fall loose and free, the ends framing her eyes and ears and jawline.

Trish was beautiful, and right now he had no idea how she was feeling about him or anything else.

"Feel better after your shower?" he said, not moving from his chair.

"I feel cleaner after a long drive. How do *you* feel, Connor?"

He deliberately misunderstood the sharp look in her eyes and the worry in her voice.

"I'm tired. We put up yards of shelves today, cutting and sanding and staining. And I'm glad to see you."

Trish took a long, deep breath, and Connor resisted the urge to watch her chest rise and fall.

"Are you? Glad to see me?"

He stood and crossed the room to stand in front of her, breathing in the fresh scent of her skin and her spicy shampoo. He kept his hands at his sides, though.

"Of course I am. Why wouldn't I be?"

"I don't know. You seem awfully comfortable here somehow."

He reached for her hand, and he was glad when she laced her fingers through his. He'd never encountered her acting...angry or jealous or uneasy before, not with him. They'd never had anything formal enough between them for that to make sense.

At least that was what he thought.

"I like it here, sure. My family's from here, I've visited my whole life. You'll see how beautiful it is for yourself tomorrow. But I'm still happy you're here."

Trish stared into his eyes again, and Connor smiled just a

little. She shook her head and stepped into his arms. He pressed his cheek against her cool, damp hair.

"Good," she said, then turned to brush her lips against his ear. Even as his body responded, he struggled to keep Laura's deep voice and soft, mountain accent out of his mind. "Because I'm glad to be here with you. Why don't you get ready for bed?"

He pulled back enough to kiss her, the peppermint of her mouthwash sharp against his lips and tongue.

And his sense of dislocation returned full force. Not only from being with Trish in Wolf Branch, which was strange enough. But the kiss itself, slow and deliberate, almost cautious, pushed him into the unknown.

He felt a chill, thinking it as her hands slowly explored his back and he gently held her face. That didn't change the fact that the two of them had always moved more quickly, with an almost hurried pace. Both acknowledging how rarely they had time together and wanting to make the most of it.

This part of their friendship had a purpose, after all. Not quite lovers, a bit more than friends. Leisurely lovemaking didn't fit the pattern.

Connor moved his hands lower, across her neck and shoulders, pulling her closer. Excitement rose within him, unfolding slowly and taking a deeper hold than usual as her breasts pushed against his chest.

He fought to keep the questions and images and impressions swirling in his mind from gaining footing.

How would all of this be different if he held Laura in his arms? Was his response slower because the one he truly wanted wasn't here?

Trish drew back, eyes closed and a tiny line between her eyebrows. She held her hands flat against his chest. When she opened her eyes, she seemed more curious than upset.

"Know what? I'm tired too, Connor. Mind if we just go to sleep?"

He did his best to hide his relief, but he couldn't pretend it wasn't strong within him.

"You sure?" He kissed the tip of her nose. "Whatever you want is fine with me. I know I could use some rest."

She nodded, and her smile was sad.

"I'm sure. Actually sleeping will be a new adventure for us, huh?"

"Okay. I'll meet you there."

He reached around her to grab his overnight bag, then went into the bathroom.

He stared into the mirror for a long time, playing back the lie he'd just told her and himself.

He wanted sleep.

He *needed* sleep.

But he doubted his restless mind would be on board with that plan any time soon.

Chapter 19

The football field and the high school and everything else looked strange enough to be unrecognizable to Laura's eyes as she leaned against her little car the next morning.

The weather had changed dramatically, for one thing. The clear blue autumn sky had disappeared, taking on the same heavy, wet cast as the fog swirling around the night before.

No, that wasn't quite right. The wispy fog had been playful, mischievous, hiding and revealing landmarks and even people as it pleased.

This sky hung low overhead, clouds dark gray and overstuffed. All the color seemed drained from the fiery display of leaves in the mountains, leaving them looking drab and dull.

She was almost convinced she could throw one of the random gravels scattered across the cracked pavement high enough to hit the clouds. Then she'd only have to duck and run to avoid the torrential rain caused when one of them gave way like a balloon.

She snorted at her runaway imagination and kicked at the pavement, pulling her gray hoodie closer around her neck. The gusty wind was cool and damp enough for something heavier, but the raincoat she kept stashed in her car wouldn't fit over a warmer jacket.

She also hadn't wanted to get into any kind of long conversation with either of her parents when she stopped by the house an hour ago. A quick shower, an even quicker breakfast of one of her mother's divine morning glory muffins, and she'd dashed out, grabbing what she could without thinking.

And coffee, of course. She took another long sip from her favorite pink thermos, grateful for her mother's heavenly brew even when she knew she'd need more to get through the day.

A set of metal double doors set into the brick of the high school slammed open, and a herd of girls trudged across the crowded parking lot, out toward one of the baseball fields beyond the off-limits football field. Laura wondered if even the much-anticipated renewal of the almighty rivalry with Laurel Gap might be either interrupted or called off by the kind of frigid downpour the leaden sky predicted.

But no one would ever risk smudging those perfect white lines just in case they managed to sneak it in before the grass turned into a mud-slick bog.

The girls wore a mix of shorts, t-shirts, sweatpants, and sweatshirts in the school's purple and gold, and most of them were obviously unhappy about their early exercise. Dragging their feet, staring at the ground in front of them, glancing uneasily up at the sky. Only a couple smiled and chatted as they walked.

If Laura remembered correctly from the vast gulf of four years ago, they'd probably do some kind of warmup on the dormant baseball field first. Jumping jacks, maybe, or even pushups or sit-ups in the thick grass. Then they'd be off to run laps around the brown track around the edge of the football field, fussing the whole time about how sweat and humid air would leave their hair a frizzy mess.

Her knees and back were still grateful for the springy surface that made the mile a lot more tolerable. Especially combined with the endless practices for marching band field shows she'd been doing at the same time. One of the many ways she and Jim had gotten to be friends all those years ago, with the band and the football team often traveling together.

She rolled her eyes and drew in a long, deep breath through her mouth, then blew it out between her pursed lips. Her mind wasn't going to play nicely today, no matter how much she needed it to.

Yes, this was the same track she'd walked around with Connor, not quite two days and a thousand years ago. The same Connor she hoped wouldn't come along for the meeting Laura had scheduled with his mother any minute now.

The text message from the town's librarian earlier that morning had dragged her out of half-sleep, the best she'd managed during the long, long night in Jim's bed that had never felt so small before. She always set only work messages to ring through overnight, but so many could safely be put off after a quick glance. This one had jolted her awake and into action.

A budget and planning meeting was no big deal, even a surprise one. But the mention of Anne Griffith's name (and the possibility of her son) made it impossible for Laura to pretend to sleep any longer.

She had the feeling Jim hadn't slept any better, even though he'd proclaimed himself too tired for sex or even talking as soon as they'd gotten to his apartment. She couldn't remember a time when he hadn't at least tried. And she couldn't pretend she hadn't been relieved when he turned onto his side away from her, and put on a good show of dropping right off.

As if thinking of Anne conjured her, the blue sedan turned into the parking lot and headed for one of the few empty spaces in front of the cannery. Not close enough to see if anyone rode in the back seat, not yet.

She pushed away from the solid mass of her much smaller car and waited, trying not to hope Connor wasn't with them. Pretending she didn't hope he *was*. A soft sigh escaped her when only Anne and Evan got out of the car.

They were all smiles as they walked toward her through all the beat and battered student vehicles. Laura did her best to look welcoming. She liked both of them very much, no matter how unsettled her feelings were about their son.

"Thank you for meeting us so early, Laura," Evan said, taking her hand in both of his. "And thank you for such a lovely dinner last night."

Laura tried not to laugh. Her mind resisted the idea that they'd sat down together on her parents' porch less than twelve hours ago.

"You're quite welcome," she said. "I'm glad you had a good time. My parents said you're welcome again whenever you're ready."

His pale blue eyes twinkled, somehow still bright under the gloomy sky.

"I get the feeling we'll be seeing a lot of your parents, and I'm truly looking forward to that. I'm off to speak to Linda and some of the other teachers. You two have a good morning."

He stepped away from Laura, kissed Anne's cheek, and ambled toward the double doors that still stood open. He pushed one closed with a flourish, then stepped through the other and closed it behind him.

Anne chuckled from beside Laura.

"He's so excited about getting started here," Anne said. "He's like a school kid himself."

"We're all thrilled to have the two of you. I hope you're both ready for the major change of pace from the city."

Laura tried not to wince at her own words. Now she sounded like Jim. But Anne only smiled.

"We're both thrilled to finally be here. This move has been years in the making." She waved toward the football field. "Walk a couple of laps with me? All this unpacking has me feeling stiff and sore."

"I'd love to, but we're scheduled to meet at the library in about fifteen minutes." Laura glanced at her watch just in time to see a message pop up. "Or, maybe we have an hour since it just got postponed."

Anne nodded once. "Perfect timing."

The girls were still occupied on the baseball field. But even if they did end up heading this way, Laura remembered dodging around track walkers many times during her own years of running laps.

She caught herself trying to sneak quick glances at Anne as they walked. Connor had her green eyes and brown hair, but his features were more like Evan's. More square and solid. Not nearly as fine or delicate.

To Laura's eye, Connor was the best possible combination of them both.

Before she could settle into the shock of that thought—and how *true* it felt to her—Anne distracted her.

"You know all about our plans, Laura, and a lot about our lives in Chicago. I'm curious about you. How do you like working for the town?"

Laura had a carefully refined answer, all about working hard and gaining experience while considering her options for going back to school at some point. An answer she'd developed to keep her grandparents, Jim, and sometimes her mother from giving her a dirty look. Or worse, a painfully long and earnest lecture about not utilizing her *potential.* Whatever that was supposed to mean.

She surprised herself by telling Anne the truth.

"You know, the longer I do it, the more I learn and see my work making a real difference, the more I love it. I'm excited to see what we can get going with the library, for example, and at our old cannery."

Anne laughed, and the light, joyful sound made Laura smile.

"See?" Anne said. "How could I help being eager to get started working with you with that kind of enthusiasm? Sounds to me like you've found a good fit. And like the town is lucky to have someone like you."

Laura managed not to snort or shake her head.

"Thank you for saying so. I hear a lot about how I should go back to school and really make something of myself. Live up to some sort of mythical potential everyone but me can see."

She glanced at Anne again, horrified that she'd said so much. Venting to Connor, someone her own age and going through the same struggles, was one thing. Running her mouth to his mother when she was supposed to be a professional representing Wolf Branch was quite another.

Thankfully Anne looked sympathetic rather than shocked.

"You sound a lot like Connor. I can see how happy he is with the work he's doing, and I think he knows it deep down. But he gets the idea from out in the world that he could be so much more if he only got out of some kind of imagined rut and got himself started. That kind of drumbeat of *advice* is hard to ignore even if you want to."

Laura bit back a reply about beautiful and ambitious Trish pushing him. Partly because she couldn't help imagining that conversation happening over at the hotel while they were both in bed. And not after *sleeping*, either.

This might be the perfect time to stay honest while she had the chance.

"That's how I've been feeling, yeah. I tell myself a lot of the same things about how I don't want to be trapped in a small town, getting roped into some kind of dead-end job that will never be anything more. But deep down, there's this whisper. I *want* to do this work. I want to make a real difference right here. Not drown in some gigantic university or corporation or huge city where I'll only be another anonymous cog no one ever knows about."

She was again surprised at how much she'd said. But even more so at how her hands shook and her heart sped up. Something about Anne made Laura want to tell the truth, no matter how hard that truth was. Even to herself.

Connor had struck her exactly the same way.

"I don't hear anything that sounds like missing out on potential," Anne said, with another of her warm smiles. "Now I know you didn't ask me, and we only just met. But you sound to me like going somewhere else might be what *drains* your potential. The excitement I hear in your voice talking about the library and the cannery. Your *joy*."

Laura laughed under her breath and looked away. They'd drawn even with the girls, now engaged in the dreaded jumping jacks. Their shouted counting at least sounded enthusiastic.

Or maybe it was only loud.

"That's it, I think," she said, looking toward the cannery and Wolf Branch tucked into its lovely little valley beyond. "Joy. I don't feel anything like that when I think of going back to school, or even moving to Charlottesville. I feel curious, sure. I thought that was what I wanted to do for a long time. Get away from here, get on with my life. But now that it's time, I think...maybe that was only what I thought I *should* do."

With those words out in the open where she couldn't pretend the feelings weren't real any more, tension drained out of Laura's jaw and neck, her arms and legs. She wanted to sink down on the bouncy brown track, maybe curl up and take a nap.

Only the approach of thumping feet and the mutter of conversation approaching from behind them stopped her.

She turned to Anne to warn her about the impending herd, and the words died in her throat.

Laura couldn't tell if it was a subtle change in the gloom overhead, or the effect of her own near-confession. But for the first time, she saw a deep sadness in Anne's eyes.

Even when she smiled, the sadness came through the warmth.

Connor didn't have that, even with the same eyes. And Laura realized she hoped he never would. She wished she could keep him from ever having that underlying sorrow, no matter what it took.

Anne gently took her arm and they both stepped to the side just as the herd thundered by.

"When it comes to joy," Anne said, "all I'll say is pay attention when you find it. We all have choices, all our lives long. Most of the time, we can't know what those choices will lead to. But I believe choosing to walk away from our own true joy is a hard mistake to overcome."

Laura tried her best to smile, but she knew the sadness in her own eyes would come through loud and clear.

She was terribly afraid she had found joy in Connor. Joy and ease and humor, and comfort she'd never known with another person.

Comfort she couldn't imagine she'd ever have with Jim.

The problem was Connor was almost certainly with

beautiful Trish right that minute, and he'd be going back to Chicago with her in another few days.

Laura didn't have the heart to ask Anne what to do if the person who brought her so much joy was the one walking away.

And she had no idea how to stop him, much less any right to try.

Chapter 20

Connor walked back through his parents' new
house with yet another huge armful of books, and stopped in
his tracks. He'd come to love this part of any building or
moving or staging project, and even more to love the way it
took him by surprise every time.

The dusty, empty, half-finished room had transformed
itself between one load of books and the next. Now he stood
in the middle of an amazing miniature library that only
needed a few last bits of tidying up.

No longer a project-in-progress in a house in transition,
this was now the heart of the home.

The home he'd helped make for his own parents.

That made the wave of satisfaction Connor always felt at
this moment a thousand times deeper and stronger.

He settled the books onto the shelves, filling a row at
about his chest height, and stepped into the middle of room.
He blinked, only then noticing an odd pattern in what he'd
thought were random arrangements of different colors and
sizes.

Spines thick or thin, made of scratchy cloth or slick

paper. Paperbacks that would fit into his pocket all the way up to huge tomes he could just about use for the foundation of another house. Some brand new, but most years or decades old. Many older than Connor himself.

He'd followed the packing order back in Chicago and the unpacking order here, thinking that was just both of his parents wanting to make sure they'd know where everything was. That was certainly true with such detailed lists and careful sorting into boxes. Even the blank shelves and spaces made a soothing kind of sense. He knew they'd be filled in over time and only enhance the subtle pattern.

But he saw more than that here, even if he couldn't quite grasp the structure or the reason for it. Something reassuring and true, movement his eyes followed, not caring that his conscious mind failed to understand.

Connor still saw it, and he knew it was good.

A sudden humming from the kitchen pulled him back into here and now, into the world where he still had a few books and a whole bunch of framed photos to unpack.

And where Trish had turned into more of a jarring element in this peaceful setting than he wanted to admit.

He'd had a rough and painfully disorienting night at the mercy of his subconscious, much like his mother often did. Every time he dropped off to sleep, he dreamt he slept beside Laura. In a bed and a house he'd never seen before, but the look and feel of it suited him as well as the woman he slept with.

Connor saw every detail and dimension of the bedroom and the other rooms and even the yard with such clarity that he was certain he built it all without a single blueprint. That house felt close and secure to him, even wide awake.

All night, more times than he cared to count, he woke with no idea where he was until he remembered going to sleep in a hotel room. And disappointment at who he shared the bed with settled itself deeper into his mind and heart every time.

He was too afraid to wonder if he'd inherited a faint echo of his mother's dreams after all.

After a quiet but companionable breakfast at the hotel, Trish had asked to see the house. A reasonable request that seemed harmless enough. She wanted to spend time with him, after all, and get to know Wolf Branch a little.

And Connor wanted to get the work done at the house before he headed back to Chicago and...

He had no idea what came after that.

Now that she was here, though, putting some kind of early lunch together with his parents' pots or pans or plates or bowls, the whole thing felt off. Ill-fitting. Like he'd taken a wrong turn a few miles back, but he hadn't yet found the place to turn around.

The idea of going back with Trish—riding with her rather than getting his own rental—felt about as pleasant as scrubbing his skin with the sandpaper they'd so carefully used on these shelves.

He shook his head and decided to switch gears from books to pictures.

The only furniture in the room so far was two huge over-stuffed wingback chairs. The burgundy thrones had sat near a row of window in his parents' apartment for as long as he could remember, in the same room where most of the books had come from. Here the windows were smaller, and they looked out not toward a city neighborhood with a distant glimpse of the lake, but over a narrow strip of yard and the autumn glow of the mountain across the road.

Each chair and the huge matching ottoman held a sturdy box marked "Library Photos" in his dad's looping handwriting. Connor opened the first and laughed out loud.

Tucked in around the metal and wooden frames was his

mom's favorite fluffy pink lap blanket. He'd helped pack these photos without that extra bit of protection. She must have added it herself before the boxes were taped up.

He pulled the blanket out, amazed as always at how soft it was. Once he draped it across the back and one arm of the chair on the right, the room felt even more like home.

"What's got you laughing out here?" Trish said from the kitchen doorway, a smile clear in her voice.

She leaned against the frame with her arms crossed, wearing a black t-shirt tucked into blue jeans. Looking like her normal happy, smart-ass self somehow, rather than road weary and so sad from the night before.

"My Mom. She had her library blanket snugged in with all these photos instead of with her clothes or other blankets. I guess no one can put it in the wrong place by accident."

"Very sensible of her." Trish walked over and touched the pink fluff. "She'd probably have a hard time replacing something this nice down here."

Connor closed his eyes for a second, struggling not to snap an ill-advised reply about perfectly good stores all around them, or "do you honestly believe the World Wide Web winks out of existence if you accidently stray south of the Chicago River?"

He wasn't sure if Trish had always been so dismissive of anything outside her world, or if he'd simply never *been* outside that world with her before.

"Listen, why don't I help you with these," she said, the little line between her eyebrows making a return appearance. "Then we can have lunch. Maybe go for a hike by the river you want me to see?"

"Sure. That sounds great. We've only got one ladder, want to hand them up to me?"

Connor escaped into the living room to get his mother's step chair before Trish could answer.

He'd stood on the lightweight contraption—more like a modified red high chair with metal legs and two extending footrests rather than a proper ladder—plenty of times as a teenager. He hoped it would hold his weight now.

"Want me to climb up instead?" Trish said, frowning at the step chair. "I'm not sure that will hold you."

"I'll be fine. I use this all the time."

He glanced at the clever little map his mother had drawn on the box like all the boxes of books, marking the doorways and windows along with where the things inside should go. He'd never seen one so sensible and clear on any moving or staging job before, but it was exactly how anyone should expect a career librarian to pack books.

Then he positioned the chair and climbed up, holding the shelf in front of him along with his breath. It wobbled a bit beneath him, but not as badly as he expected.

No doubt it made more sense for Trish to climb up. He probably outweighed her by a good forty or fifty pounds.

The truth was he could stand for her to hand him the photos. But the idea of her placing them on the shelves bothered him somehow. Like the hunches his mother so often got, that feeling was too strong to ignore.

"Who are these people?" Trish said, holding out a photo of Connor's grandfather Hurricane Ed, his Auntie Gwen and Uncle Mark, and their three rowdy sons. "I've never seen them before."

Could they have been friends all these years and not talked about Hurricane Ed, or Auntie Gwen, who often qualified as at least a tropical depression? Connor thought he'd shared those tales with pretty much everyone he knew.

"My grandfather on the Illinois side, and my aunt and uncle and cousins. I'll have to tell you about them sometime. They're quite the crew."

He put the image of a bunch of smiling faces who looked

remarkably alike on the top shelf and reached for the next. His mother and father about fifteen years ago, mid-laugh and gazing into each other's eyes, somewhere along the deep blue water of Lake Michigan.

"Those two I recognize," she said. "I hope they're happy here. It really is beautiful, just like you said. I never imagined your parents leaving the city."

Connor focused on the image, keeping his thoughts about how long his parents had been planning this move to himself.

The way they looked at each other left no doubt how they felt. They loved him, of course, and their families and many friends. But no one who ever spent time around Evan and Anne Griffith could miss how close they were, how they each seemed to orbit the other.

The contrast to how he felt about Trish even during the best of times was leaving a world of vibrant, rich color, full of sound and smell and touch and taste, and entering a flat, grainy, washed-out black and white.

All at once, he didn't want to have anything in this house that reminded him of Trish. He didn't want to look at the carefully chosen and arranged pictures and think of her helping him unpack them. He didn't even want to remember sitting at the sweet, cozy little table and having lunch with her.

Whatever role they'd played in each other's life didn't make sense any more, certainly not in a house perfectly arranged for people so very much in love.

And he couldn't stand to think of how natural he'd felt sitting beside Laura, having dinner with his family and hers. Because then Connor couldn't help thinking of how often Boyfriend Jim must have happily sat there instead, and would from here on out.

"I'm not sure about where these should go after all," he

lied, climbing down with both photographs in his hand. "I'll ask Mom and Dad later. How about we pack up lunch and head on down to the river instead?"

Trish smiled, but that sad little wrinkle never left her forehead.

"Okay, Connor. I want to be sure to see that before I leave. Then we'll see how it goes from there."

Chapter 21

The Wolf Branch Public Library had been one of Laura's favorite places since she was old enough to toddle across the broad porch of the grand old Victorian house.

The original family's wealth came from the same railroad that brought the town to life nearly a hundred and fifty years ago. No one knew for certain why they'd decided to dress the elaborate woodwork of the exterior in a striking combination of purple and gold with black accents, but no one would ever dream of changing the colors now.

Other buildings and businesses across town—including the high school's sports and academic teams—had adopted the color scheme as their own.

Inside the library, great efforts had been made to preserve the historic character of the donated house. Floors and staircases and all manner of decorative trim were kept polished and gleaming, and rows of shelves filling the many rooms were built to match.

Reading nooks retained the original furniture as long as it held up, and even today a few curvy chairs with elaborate velvet upholstery remained. Updates to the kitchen and bathrooms had been made carefully, along with adding additional electrical and electronic capability.

Laura hadn't been the only one to breathe a sigh of relief when network cables that managed to snarl and look awful no matter how carefully managed had been removed more than ten years ago in favor of invisible wireless systems.

She waited in one of the library's tiny square meeting rooms now, summoned there by Jim's text message only a few minutes before. More like interrupted by his message, and relocated by her own reply of needing to talk to him. The sooner the better.

The meeting room was awash in rich purple, with paint on the walls and velvet curtains on one window and even a round rug over the hardwood floor. A narrow table with delicate spindly legs, probably original to the house, sat under the window.

Laura couldn't imagine putting anything as heavy as books or certainly her elbows on the dainty thing. So instead she did her best to relax in a modern office chair; the black leather, wheeled base, and mesh back comfortable but jarringly modern in the space.

She distracted herself by wondering what this room's purpose had been, decades before small study groups or meetings of under five people crowded inside. One wall was covered with built-in shelves jammed full of books, mostly history of Wolf Branch and the region. That and the ground floor location near the street didn't make much sense for a bedroom.

She decided it had been a dedicated reading room for the lady of the house, barely wide enough for her fashionably vast skirts. Built with love to give her a much-needed bit of privacy from her hectic day raising the seven children who'd grown up here.

Laura was trying to imagine getting married at seventeen

the way that lady had, and living in the same house with the same man for decades, when someone knocked on the six-panel door.

"Hey Laura," Jim said, walking in and closing the door behind him. "You look like you're a thousand miles away."

He rolled another modern chair close to her and sat, without a kiss or a touch. From the damp edges of his hair, he'd taken the time to shower after his online classes. He'd even replaced the t-shirt and sweatpants with jeans and a golf shirt.

"I'm right here," Laura said. "Only a hundred years in the past. Classes go okay?"

"You know they did. You're right. I could sleep through these." He shook his head. "I'm sorry I was kind of a jerk about it yesterday."

Laura reached out to take his hand and ended up patting it instead.

"Thanks, but I'm about to take over the role of jerk."

She took a deep breath and forced herself to look into his eyes. She was more relieved than she wanted to admit that he seemed more resigned than upset.

"Go ahead," he said, one side of his mouth lifting. "It's all right."

Laura reminded herself how long they'd known each other, how many breakups they'd each seen the other go through. It was no wonder at all that he at least suspected what was coming.

"You should go on to Charlottesville, Jim. Don't wait for me, because I'm not going. I don't know what I'm going to do yet, but whatever it is won't be there."

He nodded, never looking away from her eyes.

"And it won't be with me. Can you tell me something? Please?"

She nodded herself and tried to smile.

"You know I can. I doubt either one of us are planning to yell and scream and refuse to ever speak to each other again. I hope not, anyway."

"Is it because of this new guy? Connor?"

Laura sighed, trying not to think of Anne still chatting with the librarians a few doors away. How her words about joy had made this tense conversation with Jim necessary sooner rather than a distant but inevitable someday.

Or about how Laura would be hard pressed to avoid seeing Connor (and maybe beautiful Trish) before he finally left for Chicago in a few days time.

"Not really," she said, running her hands along the padded arms of her chair. "I think you and I were headed this way before now, don't you? Even if it *was* about him, he's leaving in a few days anyway. Does that make a difference?"

Jim shrugged, and when he reached for her hand she let him take it.

"I don't know. Right now I don't like the guy very much, to tell you the truth. I might if I ever actually talked to him. But even if we *were* headed this way, I hate the idea of you being sad and alone no matter what."

Laura laced her fingers through his. "So do I. But making you wait to go start your own life when I know I can't go with you is more than I can stand. Boring classes this morning aside, you love what you're studying. I see how you light up when you talk about it."

Jim rolled his eyes and shook his head, and all at once Laura missed the easy friendship between them. She had a feeling she wouldn't miss their romantic relationship nearly as much.

"Yeah, I get excited about politics of all things." He tried to look embarrassed, but the fire still came through in his eyes. The *joy*. "Kind of weird to base my life on getting deeper into that."

"No, you love it and you're good at it. We need people who love politics to get involved instead of people who are only after power. If you want to talk weird, I'm considering staying put right here in Wolf Branch. Getting deeper into *small town* management, and all the politics that go with it. Like I always said I wouldn't."

Jim squeezed her hand, and his relaxed smile let her know it all made sense to him now.

"You've made a big difference already, Laura. The town is lucky to have you. Some other guy will be too. Even if it does turn out to be Connor."

He pulled her to her feet and into a hug. Laura let out a long, shuddering breath, but she was determined not to cry.

"You okay?" she said as they moved apart.

He winked. "You know me. I'll miss you, but I'll land on my feet. Are *you* okay?"

"I will be. Keeping busy won't be a problem. The rest will work itself out eventually."

He turned toward the door, then looked back over his shoulder.

"I wouldn't be so sure he's leaving. Connor, I mean. I saw the way he looked at you last night."

Laura stared down at her feet, trying to ignore the sinking in her stomach. She'd seen the way Connor and Trish walked with their arms around each other, too.

"I appreciate you saying that, Jim. I guess we'll see what happens. Take care."

She looked up just in time to see him smile and wink at her as he walked out the door.

Laura sank back into the chair, wiping away a couple of tears that managed to escape after all. It wouldn't do to look like she'd been crying when it was time to drive Anne back over to the high school to meet Evan.

And it certainly wouldn't do to look all-to-pieces if she did see Connor, today or before he left.

She wished she could borrow a little of Jim's confidence, about Connor or herself or anything else.

At the moment, getting through the rest of the day without dissolving into a puddle of tears felt like about the best she could hope for.

Chapter 22

Even though the tension across his neck and shoulders had eased considerably, Connor's sense of displacement remained strong, sitting in Trish's rental car beside the high school and the cannery. A picnic lunch of surprisingly good ham sandwiches and a long hike along the river left him feeling pleasantly tired.

What should have been a difficult conversation with Trish left him feeling sad, but somehow not nearly so tied up in indecisive knots.

Heavy clouds threatened to put a damper on tonight's big football game that even his city boy soccer-playing self knew everyone in town was excited about. His parents were discussing attending themselves if it didn't turn into a downpour.

Something about community spirit and rivalries and such.

Connor had no intention of going with them no matter what the weather turned out to be. Too much chance of running into Laura and Boyfriend Jim cheering on their shared alma mater.

He had more than enough trouble with his jumbled-up feelings about Laura and Trish and everything else without trying to deal with that.

"You don't have to leave today, Trish," he said. "You just got here last night."

She brushed a stubborn lock of hair back over her ear, staring out at the football field as her hair flipped back onto her cheek.

"I think we're both ready for me to go. I drove down here to surprise you, remember? I'd say we both have more than enough surprise to deal with for now. Even though I think it will all turn out for the best, it's definitely enough for me."

He stopped himself from reaching for her, maybe tucking her hair back into place.

"I've known you too long to bother trying to argue with you. Let me know when you get off the road for the night, when you get back home?"

She turned and smiled at him. Not her usual confident, flirty smile, but honest enough to relieve a bit of his worry.

"I will. I might make a few stops along the way, see what the world is like outside the city while I have the chance. Speaking of chance, what do you think the odds are that you'll come back to Chicago anytime soon?"

"I don't know. I don't know much of anything right now. I am going to miss you."

Trish leaned over and kissed his cheek.

"I'll miss you, too. We were a good match until now, huh? What did they call it years ago, friends with benefits?"

Connor laughed harder than he meant to, and after a second Trish joined in.

"Would you believe that's exactly what my Mom said about us?" he said. "She thought it was a good thing."

"It was, Connor. It was."

This time she touched his cheek, and brushed her lips

against his. He took the hint and his chance to escape, grabbing his overnight bag and stepping out of the car.

"Have a good drive, Trish. Talk to you later."

She backed out the second he closed the door and drove away without looking back.

Connor breathed in the damp, chilly air, smelling of wood smoke and rain on the way. He slowly walked toward his parents' car, parked in the same spot as when they'd arrived only a couple of days ago. Days that had somehow upended the course of his life.

Had they, though? Really?

He still didn't want to go back for a master's degree, or work in architecture at all. He still wanted to *build* things. Learn as much as he could, get as much experience as he could manage.

Maybe eventually go for his contractor's license, like Laura had suggested that first day, walking about the track in the bright sunshine.

Now no one walked or ran or lingered outside at all.

Just gray sky and blustery wind and general gloom.

He set his bag on the cracked pavement and leaned against the chilly side of his parents' car, not wanting to wander around the high school and disturb classes during the school day. He had no idea where Linda's classroom was, or even if that's who his parents were talking to.

Or was his mother somewhere else? His jumbled mind couldn't put the details of the early morning phone call back together again.

Didn't matter, really. He wasn't overly fit for conversation or polite company at the moment anyway.

And he had no idea what he'd say if anyone actually tried to talk to him.

Going back to Chicago made sense, going by his default plan. The one that included eventually going back to school.

The one made by other people more than by him.

Leaving Wolf Branch made sense, too. Not because he didn't like being here. He truly did. More than he'd realized during quick visits as a snotty city kid eager to get back home. The town and the mountains and the pace of life felt good to him now. Like he could really settle in and be at home.

The idea of being close to his parents didn't hurt, either.

But the reality of running into Laura, at least until she left for Charlottesville with Boyfriend Jim, did hurt. More than he wanted to admit.

Almost as much as the idea of never seeing her again.

Because Laura *did* make sense.

She suited him, somehow. Fit him. That might seem crazy to someone who didn't live in his head with the short time they'd known each other. But none of that made it less true.

Or made him less certain she felt the same way, at least when they were together.

He closed his eyes and turned away at a fierce gust of gritty wind from the football field, wishing he could turn away from the thoughts in his head, too.

Laura might very well be caught up in the same kind of expectations and plans as he was. Or as he had been, since he felt like he was drifting on the unknown right now. But she might be unable—or unwilling—to set herself adrift the way he had.

He opened his eyes as the wind settled down, just as Laura's little white car parked a few spaces away. His mother sat in the passenger seat, speaking to Laura before she got out of the car and smiled at Connor. Laura slowly got out as his mom reached his side.

"I didn't expect to see you here, son. Where's Trish?"

"She left, Mom. Right before you got here. I think we both had a few too many surprises."

His mother rubbed his back the same way she had when he was a little boy, upset over a stubbed toe or broken toy, or an early broken heart that truly did feel like the end of the world.

"I hear people talk about their twenties being the best years of their lives," she said. "But that never made sense to me. Or your father, or a bunch of other people who are willing to be honest about it. I wish I could kiss it and make it better, but I can't. Life will get better on its own, if you let it."

Connor put his arm around her, remembering the stories he'd heard about how rough her teens and twenties had been. Struggles with addiction, mental and emotional trouble. To the point that she'd been in hospitals and rehab before she found the peace and calm that were such a fundamental part of her.

And here he was moping about whether he wanted to continue his already fine education, along with the depressingly common issue of a little relationship trouble.

One glance at Laura waiting by her car had his heart informing him loud and clear this wasn't the usual trouble.

"Thanks, Mom. Want to get in the car and out of this wind?"

She laughed and shook her head.

"I'm glad to finally be here, but I'm going to miss the cool wind blowing off the lake in Chicago. This feels wonderful to me. I think I'll go inside and join your father, though. See what kinds of mischief he's getting up to."

She didn't quite look mischievous herself, but her eyes held a light that let Connor know she understood she was leaving him alone with Laura. And she wasn't hesitating to do it.

He took a deep breath of the freshening wind that smelled more like rain by the minute. He was going to miss the breeze over Lake Michigan himself, but maybe not quite enough to go back.

When he turned Laura was already standing beside him. She was as beautiful in the stormy gray light as she had been in the autumn sun, but he couldn't pretend she didn't look as weary and heartsore as he felt.

They both spoke at the same time and then laughed, because nothing else could possibly have happened.

"You go ahead," he said. "I forgot Mom had a meeting at the library this morning until just now."

"She did, it went really well. Everyone's amazed at the things she wants to do in our little town. And I'm not the only one who believes she'll get every bit of it done."

"Oh, she will. She's a force of nature when she sets her mind to something. Thank you for making them both feel so welcome. Me too."

Laura looked away, across the muted green of the football field.

"My pleasure. Kinda wondering if they'll manage to get the big game in tonight. Feels like it's going to storm."

Connor watched her, trying to memorize the angle of her nose, the curve of her lips. The way the wind played with her curly blonde hair, as he wondered how it would feel against his fingers.

"Mom and Dad were talking about coming down to watch if it's not too bad. We were more of a soccer family when I was growing up. The other football, you might say. Big in the Midwest, not so much in the South. You planning to watch tonight?"

She shook her head.

"I saw more than enough football when I was going to high school here. The marching band had to go to every single home game, and more away games than made sense with long drives through the mountains."

The images in his mind of a younger Laura in a cheerleader's short skirt shifted to a purple and gold band uniform, and he found he liked that even more.

"Yeah? What did you play? I fancied myself a bass player for a while until I realized just how bad the callouses were going to get."

She turned and looked at him with a strange smile.

"A good friend of mine played guitar and complained about the same thing. I played tenor sax."

Connor smiled back, trying to ignore the mental movie changing yet again, now featuring her in a slinky black dress in some bar in Chicago with a saxophone.

Those dreams of her had worked deeper into his mind that he thought.

Realizing she was probably talking about Boyfriend Jim playing guitar finally drove the fantasy out of his head.

"Did you play in college? Saxophone? I wasn't good enough at soccer to do more than games for fun."

She shrugged, and the corners of her mouth turned down.

"For the first couple of years. Then I got too busy. I miss it sometimes."

"Maybe you can pick it up again in Charlottesville." He swore in his mind, trying not to scowl. No matter what happened—or didn't happen—between them, the last thing he wanted to do was join the chorus of people pushing Laura where she didn't want to go. "If you decide you want to move there, I mean."

She stared up at the sky for a few seconds, and when she looked into his eyes she was blinking back tears, but her expression was strong. Determined.

"I'm not going to Charlottesville. I decided...well, pretty much today. After talking to your mother as a matter of fact."

"My mother? How did that... Wait, never mind. That's none of my business. She's a great one to talk to, about anything."

Laura took a deep breath and held it, while Connor struggled to stop himself from asking whether *Jim* was still leaving. And when. And how Laura might feel about that.

"I'm sure you'll miss talking to her," Laura said, talking too fast. "You know, when you head back up north."

Chapter 23

Laura did everything she could to keep breathing through her nose, refusing to look away from Connor's green eyes no matter how badly she wanted to. She was terribly afraid if she let out the gasp her lungs were demanding, the tears she'd been fighting back would follow.

Forcing herself to mention the idea of Connor leaving had taken a hell of a lot out of her. Far more than watching Jim walk away.

But something about the way Anne had rubbed his back, and the shadows around his eyes and face right now, drove her to do it anyway.

Beautiful Trish nowhere in sight hadn't hurt. Laura reminded herself that any number of things could explain her absence.

Even though a decidedly masculine overnight bag sat on the pavement at Connor's feet. If he was planning to stay at the hotel again tonight with Trish, that didn't really make sense

"I don't know what I'm going to do, Laura. About going back to Chicago or school or work or anything else. But I'm sure I'll want to talk to my parents about it." He paused, leaned back against the car, and shoved his hands deep into his pockets. He watched his own feet kicking at a few scattered bits of loose pavement. "Talking to you about it a few days ago helped, too."

Laura couldn't stop a sad laugh, or the little gasp that followed. She managed to stop the tears, barely.

"You sure about that?" she said. "I haven't known you all that long, but you look about as far from happy as I feel right now."

He raised his hands out to the sides, then let them fall back.

"Happy isn't the word I'd use, no. Maybe I've had too many surprises over the past few days for that. Good and bad and strange. But I feel...clearer, I think. Like some of the distractions are gone. I still don't know what I want to do, but I might be able to start figuring that out."

Laura closed her eyes, not wanting to let the faint spark of hope get started in her chest.

Did he mean Trish had turned into a distraction?

And did he mean she was gone, too? Out of Wolf Branch, and maybe out of his life?

Like Jim was out of hers?

All at once, Laura had had enough of talking in circles and trying to take such care with everyone else's feelings. Trying to coddle and cushion and protect her own feelings didn't make a whole lot more sense with the painful twists of the past few days, either.

"Where does meeting me fall on your list, Connor? Good, bad, or strange?"

He looked at her and sighed, tilting his head to the side.

"Meeting you has been strange," he said with a faint smile. "I won't pretend it hasn't. I don't know how, or why, but something about you changed something in me. And meeting you, talking with you, spending not nearly as much time as I'd *like* to with you, has been really, really good."

The hope in Laura's chest stepped forward and demanded she pay attention. No matter how scary that might be.

"Meeting you has been good too. I'd miss you if you went back up north."

Connor took a step closer. He didn't touch her or even reach out, but his gaze carried a weight and substance all its own.

"And if I didn't go back? If I've been thinking about staying in Wolf Branch instead?"

Laura checked inside before she responded, making sure how she felt rather than worrying about him or anyone else.

Except one person.

"What does Trish think about that idea? You staying here?"

Connor raised his eyebrows but didn't move away.

"Trish is on her way back to Chicago right now. Nothing especially bad about *that* surprise for either of us. Just a little sadness. We both figured out whatever we had wasn't working any more, so it was time to move on."

"Sounds familiar," Laura said. "A lot like a conversation I had about an hour ago. Jim's probably making arrangements right now to leave for Charlottesville the second he graduates. And that's exactly what he should do."

"So where does that leave us, then? A couple of newly single people with no earthly idea what to do next about much of anything. We're quite the pair, huh?"

Laura reached out herself, and squeezed tight when Connor took her hand. His touch felt like stepping into a warm bubble bath on a cold rainy night.

"Maybe we should figure out what to do instead of waiting for the answers to come to us," she said. "Meeting you changed something in me too. I don't want to march in place any more, waiting for all my life's choices to become perfectly clear. Waiting for someone to tell me what's best for me. I want to work that out for myself. Even if it hurts sometimes."

Connor smiled, and Laura saw his face and his whole body relax. The same way it had when he admitted he didn't want to go back to school a few incredibly short days before.

He reached for her other hand and she took his gladly.

"I don't know if I'm best for anything or anyone," he said. "Not even myself. Not yet. But I *want* to be what's best for you. That's what I want to figure out. The rest will work itself into place if I can get that part right. Will you let me figure that out, starting right this second?"

She laughed and stepped into his arms like coming home, her heart pounding alongside his.

And coming home was exactly how Connor Griffith felt to every joyful part of her.

"We can *both* figure that out. That's what I want." She drew back enough to see his face. "Sure you won't get bored in our little mountain town after your big city life?"

He grinned and cupped her cheek with his big warm hand, fingertips in her hair.

"With you around? I can't imagine anything about my life will ever feel boring again."

"Not if I can help it."

Ignoring the first big cold drops of rain falling around them, Laura reached up and pulled Connor into a kiss that made it clear how much they'd both been missing.

And a piece of the puzzle of her life slipped gracefully into place.

ABOUT KARI

Kari and her husband Jason A. Adams met in a computer lab in college in 1990 and proceeded to live out several enduring romance tropes, including rebound romance, friends into lovers, young love, and even second chance romance when they divorced and remarried, all before the end of the 90s. So it was perhaps inevitable they'd both end up writing romance.

Kari also writes fantasy, science fiction, and contemporary fiction, and she's happiest when she surprises herself. She lives at the end of a long dirt road in the middle of the woods with Jason, various house critters, and wildlife they're better off not knowing more about.

The Confidential Adventure Club

For Kari's exclusive free After The End stories and deleted scenes, discounts, early pre-sale releases, adorable pet photos, and a whole lot more not available anywhere else, visit The Confidential Adventure Club at www.smarturl.it/c-a-club.

Hope to see you there!

www.karikilgore.com
www.spiralpublishing.net

ALSO BY KARI KILGORE

I hope you enjoyed *Storms of the Heart* as much as I enjoyed writing it. For the story of how Connor's parents and their decidedly darker romance, dig into *Dreaming the Storm*: Book One of the post-apocalyptic *Storms of Future Past Series*. The story of Laura and Connor's family continues in book two, *Joining the Storm*.

For more romance stories from both me and Jason A. Adams, my real-life partner in romance, visit Spiral Publishing's Romance page at www.spiralpublishing.net/book-tag/romance.

Be the first to know about release dates and check out more of my fiction, including almost every genre with plenty of romantic elements, at www.karikilgore.com.

The Confidential Adventure Club

Want more fiction from Kari, including stories, discounts, and box sets not available anywhere else? Want to hear about locations, research, and other cool things that inspired this story and beyond? Want all that and adorable pet photos, too?

Join The Confidential Adventure Club and get a thank you gift of a free short story and a whole lot more at www.smarturl.it/c-a-club.

Hope to see you there!

The Storms of Future Past Series:

Dreaming the Storm

Joining the Storm

Into the Storm

Fighting the Storm

Sensing the Storm: A Storms of Future Past Prequel Story

Storms of Future Past Books One through Four Collection

The Voices through Time Series:

Songs in the Mountain

Secrets in the Land

Walking the Ghosts: A Voices through Time Novella

Dispatches from the Galaxy Stories:

Restricted Species

The Becalmed

The Garbage Belt

Terminalia Short Stories:

Terminalia

Little Five

Novels:

Until Death

The Dream Thief

Hand Me Downs

Plurapod Pathogen

Novellas:

Legacy of the Land

In the Pines

DNA Never Lies

Collections:

Fantastic Women: A Dark Fantasy Novella Trio

Fantastic Shorts: Volume 1

Near Future Forward (with Jason A. Adams)

Fantastic Shorts: Volume 2

Short Stories:

Intentions, The Seeds of Love, Wicked Bone, The Sound of Murder, Reflections, The Last Dragonkeeper, The Earworms, Odds and Endings, Dawn Visitor, The Spider Who Ate the Elephant, The Worry Trap, An Adventure Well Begun, Morning Glory, The Heart Is the Strongest, The Sweetest Trouble, Happily Ever After in KrampusLand, The Real Treasure in Cairo